TWO WAY CUT

PETER TURNBULL was born in Rotherham, Yorkshire, but now lives in Glasgow. He has had a variety of jobs, including steelworker and crematorium attendant, but for the past twelve years he has been a social worker, working in Sheffield, London, Glasgow, and – under an exchange programme – Brooklyn, New York.

Peter Turnbull is the author of five acclaimed crime novels set in Glasgow: *Deep and Crisp and Even*, *Dead Knock*, *Fair Friday*, *Big Money* and *Two Way Cut*, and a thriller, *The Claws of the Gryphon*. His next crime novel will be *Condition Purple*.

by the same author

Big Money
Fair Friday
Dead Knock
Deep and Crisp and Even
The Claws of the Gryphon

PETER TURNBULL

Two Way Cut

FONTANA/Collins

First published in Great Britain by William Collins Sons
& Co. Ltd, 1988
First published in Fontana Paperbacks 1989

Printed and bound in Great Britain
by William Collins Sons & Co. Ltd, Glasgow

Chapter One

Monday, 1st April, 03.00 hours.

She had fallen quiet. Then, eventually, but only eventually, she seemed to slumber.

There had been bar brawls, there had been street brawls, there had been car smashes. There had been a murder; the man had been found by a neighbour, still sobbing over the body of his wife, the knife still in his hand. He remained sobbing as the knife was eased from his grip and as he was led gently down the common stair and into the police van. There had been break-ins with nothing there but a shattered pane of glass and a jangling burglar bell by the time the cops arrived. Sometimes there wasn't even a broken pane of glass just a jangling alarm ringing in the still night keeping the tenements awake. In time, Glasgow had fallen silent. It was an eerie, tense silence, which at once calmed and unnerved the man as he walked. He was calmed by the stillness, yet unnerved because of the sense that the wrong noise, the wrong movement, could, and probably would, disturb the city and make her rise up, snarling.

The man was a cop. He was just thirty minutes away from discovering the body of the headless man.

The rain dripped from his black cape as he walked his beat, walking softly down Maryhill Road from Summerston towards St George's. He glanced at his watch: 03.00. April was just three hours old and rain fell steadily out of a windless blackness. He watched the rain fall across the glow of the street sodium lamps and continued walking, softly.

He walked past the small shops, the video libraries, the cycle shops, the second-hand furniture shops. He turned off Maryhill Road briefly, to check on the doors and windows of the post office. He'd done it once already that shift, but he was passing, it was a vulnerable building and needed regular checking. He switched on his torch and played the beam over the windows, all intact, none open, just as they had been when he was last here, before midnight, shortly before attending the domestic murder in Summerston. He swept the building from end to end with the beam of his torch and, as he did so, noticed how the rain seemed to be falling almost vertically.

He walked back on to Maryhill Road and crossed the Bilsland Drive/Queen Margaret Drive intersection. On his left were other small shop units and recently renovated houses, a sign that the concept of the 'West End' of the city was expanding northwards to embrace the Maryhill Corridor. On his right was the sunken landscaped football pitch, the floodlight poles standing like huge dark stalks reaching into the night. Further on, Maryhill Road turned to the left and assumed a decline towards Queen's Cross.

It was on the gap site at Queen's Cross that Phil Hamilton would discover the body of the headless man.

Phil Hamilton continued his beat, past the small petrol-filling station, to the beginnings of the Queen's Cross tenemental development, the collection of small shops, the dairies, the laundry, the grocers, the undertaker, the Rennie Mackintosh church, the Welfare Department building, new and squat, the old school, tall and forbidding and empty. The rain fell with an incessant hiss and the rain water gurgled in torrents in the gutter.

They were the only sounds he could hear.

Phil Hamilton was twenty-four years old. He'd been a constable in the Strathclyde Police for nearly five years. He had fallen in well with the routine and the discipline, but there was one point of professional conduct that he still had to lick. He was a smoker and once in a while he needed to draw on a nail. Whether he was on duty or not.

Right then he was on duty. Right then he needed a smoke. Badly.

He stepped off the pavement and walked on to the gap site in front of the old school. It was a dark night and once outside the spill of the street lamps he believed he wouldn't be noticed. He lit up as he walked, inhaling deeply, thankfully, cupping his hands round the tip of the nail to shield the glow. He enjoyed the smoke. It tasted pleasant in his mouth and he felt easier in himself.

Then he saw the white mound. It was in itself nothing to be suspicious of. He was well aware that gap sites tend to become large rubbish tips, and the white mound was, he thought, likely to be a plastic bag full of refuse. Perhaps two or three bags lying together.

Hamilton ambled towards it, picking his way across the rubble, his motivation being the need to justify his presence on the waste ground rather than curiosity about the exact nature of the white mound. He took his time; he still had more than half a good nail to savour.

He was a cop, a cop of modest yet respectable experience. He had seen human corpses before. Sometimes they can look just like a person sleeping, sometimes they are bloody and misshapen and have to be shovelled off the surface of the road, sometimes they are in an advanced state of decomposition and it is difficult to believe that they had once been recognizable as members of the human race. Sometimes they are found still taking their last breath and are seen to turn grey as life leaves them. Phil Hamilton was not a stranger to the human corpse and, as he approached the white mound, his suspicion became slowly, gradually, aroused and he began to feel a gnawing emptiness in the pit of his stomach.

When he was twenty-five feet away he switched on his flashlight. He saw that it was the corpse of a man, the white mound being the trunk of his body, covered by a sheet. Hamilton was later to talk of the time he discovered the headless man, and while it was true that the man's head seemed to have been hacked from his body, it had not been removed so much as re-sited. After death it sat on his chest, on top of the sheet, just above his midriff. It was half turned towards Hamilton; the eyes were open; that made it worse, the eyes being open. Hamilton looked into the dead man's eyes; they held his stare inviting a horrific fascination. The eyes were locked in an expression of shock, the mouth frozen in a half grin, it stood in the beam of his torch with the rain running down. Hamilton unbuttoned his cape and clutched his radio which was attached to the collar of his tunic. He pressed the 'send' button and said, 'Two-four-six, control, over.'

As he listened to the radio crackle he thought that he never learned, this incident not being the first time that he had wandered away from the public thoroughfare in search of a quiet, secluded place in which to enjoy a cigarette and, in doing so, discovering a dead body. He turned back towards the body, drawn by some morbid fascination, not being able to help himself staring at it, in much the same way as when he once attended the funeral of two firemen who had been killed on duty, he could not help himself looking at the dead men's colleagues, also mourners, who had escaped the conflagration that claimed the two firemen, but had nonetheless been horribly disfigured by the flames. Then he turned the other way to the string of lights on the far side of the canal. They seemed to go off and then on again, one after the other.

Somebody was running along the canal towpath. Then he caught a glimpse of the figure as the canal towpath came briefly into the spill of the sodium lamps on Garscube Road. It seemed a slight figure to Hamilton, it ran with hunched shoulders and quick scurrying steps.

'Well, not running, Sarge,' said Hamilton, struggling for words, 'sort of . . .'

'Well, laddie,' said Sussock. 'What then?'

'Scurrying.'

'Scurrying?'

'Scurrying,' said Hamilton, noting how the revolving blue lights on the roofs of the police vehicles picked out the lines on the face of the elderly detective-sergeant for a split second before plunging him into darkness again for a full second before another brief, blue illumination. 'Well, to put it another way, Sarge, the figure wasn't running like the marathon runners would run, it was taking short rapid steps, didn't have a big stride, and . . .'

'And?'

'Well, it was difficult to be certain from this distance, but I thought the shoulders were hunched up.'

'Did you shout after it?'

'No, Sarge, too far away.'

'You didn't go after it?'

'No, Sarge, I thought it inadvisable to leave the corpse. I did radio the information to the panda car.'

'I know.' Sussock nodded. 'Oscar Delta Foxtrot investigated but saw nothing.' He turned and looked to his left. Dr Din, the Sikh police surgeon, knelt by the body and then rose and covered it with an orange sheet. He stepped away from the corpse and over the white ribbon which hung from four metal stakes which had been hammered into the ground around the corpse. Access to the body was restricted to a route along a narrow path marked with stakes and white ribbon leading from the corpse directly to the nearest point of the pavement.

'A formality as you said, Sergeant,' said Dr Din. 'Yes, he is dead, most certainly.'

'Thank you, sir.' Sussock nodded at the slightly built Sikh, a turban, a raincoat, a black bag. 'It was a formality we have to observe. I'll ask the pathologist to attend now.'

'I shall return to the police station and write my report. Good night.'

'Good night, doctor,' said Sussock.

Dr Din walked down the pathway between the white ribbon towards the point where a sergeant of the uniformed branch and six constables stood awaiting instructions. There were three police vehicles in attendance, each with a blue revolving light. Behind the third police vehicle was a dark blue van despatched at the request of the police from the mortuary in Brunswick Place. Two grim-faced men sat in the mortuary van, smugly keeping out of the rain, irreverently smoking cigarettes and scanning the early morning edition of the *Daily Record*.

Sussock was aware of Hamilton standing in front of him, awaiting, like the constables on the pavement, further instruction, sir. Sussock was aware of the need to issue a command, to be seen to be in control. He had observed the procedure for cordoning off the body, what now? What now? Finally he turned to the sergeant of the uniformed branch and asked that the police constables be stationed around the perimeter of the gap site until more men could be drafted in to sweep the area. Only then did he notice the lights that had been switched on in the tenements which overlooked the gap site, only then did he notice people in their pyjamas leaning out of open windows, peering at the spectacle of police vehicles, a squad of policemen, of something on the waste ground covered by an orange sheet and surrounded by white ribbon. Only then did he notice one or two people, there's always one or two, who had left the tenements and were walking as close as they could to the police vehicles pretending to be passers-by, and as they walked would turn to their relatives and friends who were leaning out of the windows and snigger at their own antics.

In the south side of the city of Glasgow a man and his wife lay sleeping, side by side. They owned a large house which stood in its own grounds, they had two children and all slept soundly because of the locks on the windows and doors and because of Gustav the St Bernard who was allowed the run of the ground floor each and every night. Often, thought the woman, occasionally thought the man, any intrusion into their home was always by the telephone, as indeed it was that rainy night, the first in April. The telephone, a modern lightweight design of carbon black plastic, favoured by the couple for its soft, almost purring sound, rang only twice before the man groped for it with a sinewy arm, lifted the receiver, held it to his head under the blankets and murmured, 'Reynolds.' But it was enough to wake his wife, who once awake knew she would not sleep again that night. She opened her eyes and glanced at the clock on her bedside table; it was 03.45. She shut her eyes, listening to the rain fall against the windowpane and she listened as her husband talked softly and economically until he gently replaced the telephone receiver on its rest. She felt him ease out of the bed and tiptoe out of the room to dress. She knew he was sincere in his desire not to wake her, so Janet Reynolds lay still and silent with her eyes shut until she heard him leave their home. Then she too rose from her bed and pulled on her housecoat and pushed her feet into her slippers. She went downstairs. She let the slobbering tail-wagging Gustav out into the back garden and percolated some coffee. It was 04.00, by the pine-encased clock above the breakfast bar. She now had four uninterrupted hours before the children had to be up. In the drawing-room she curled up in an armchair with a historical romance open on her lap and both hands holding the mug of coffee. She began to immerse herself in the huge tome, enjoying the aroma of ground coffee and reflecting that suffering partial insomnia was not by any means without its compensations.

'Odd sense of humour,' said Reynolds, peeling back the sheet of orange polythene with one hand while holding his umbrella above his head with the other.

'I'm sorry, sir?' said Sussock. His collar was pulled up and the rain dripped from the rim of his trilby.

'The person who put the head on the chest. I think it took an odd sense of humour to do that, but I'm a pathologist, not a psychiatrist.'

'Indeed, sir.'

'Right, then.' Reynolds examined the corpse. 'What do we have? One male apparently aged between thirty and fifty, Caucasian extraction. Head separated from trunk.' Reynolds ran his fingers gently over the bones of the neck. 'Well, I'll be able to say for certain later, but the bone splinters indicate that the head was hacked off.'

'Well, how else . . .' Then Sussock coughed. 'I'm sorry, I didn't mean to sound . . .'

'It's quite all right, Sergeant. I mean hacked as opposed to being sawn. I wonder, Constable – ' Reynolds spoke to Hamilton who was standing behind Sussock – 'I wonder if you could shine the beam of your torch just here near my hand, that's it. Yes, you see the bones of the neck, the spinal column, have been severed neatly, the minor bones at the side of the neck and the tissue around the throat are both a little more tattered and torn. One blow killed him outright coming from the rear and managed to nearly, just nearly, carry his head off, but the final separation was achieved only after hacking away the bones and tissue towards the front of the throat. The look of shock on the face is significant. He wasn't expecting it, unlike a guillotine victim for example, and he was alive and conscious at the moment the blow was struck.'

'Not drugged or anything?' Sussock said to confirm the pathologist's statement for his own edification.

'No, alive and kicking. There's no other indication of injury, nothing apparent in these conditions anyway. I'll not be able to say for certain until I get him back to the laboratory.' Reynolds lifted the left arm of the cadaver and let it fall. 'Just a slight stiffening,' he said, reaching into his bag which he had laid beside him. He took a thermometer from a slender leather pouch and held it in the beam of Hamilton's torch, watching the mercury slide down the tube until it reached three degrees above freezing. 'Didn't think it was as cold as that. Thank you, Constable.' Hamilton switched off his torch and Reynolds replaced the thermometer in the leather pouch.

Sussock coughed. His chest hurt, the winters did that to him, the thin air got into his lungs and pierced them with a sharp jabbing pain. Each winter seemed worse than the last; the pain, he well knew, was the legacy of a lifetime's smoking and he had kicked the habit only after all the damage had been done. It was one more hole he'd dug for himself. 'Could you give an indication of the time of death, sir?' He spoke only because he had found that speaking eased the pain.

'All in good time, Sergeant,' said Reynolds. 'All in good time, but I would say that he was cooled about six hours ago, say about ten o'clock yesterday evening. I would also guess that he was brought here soon after that because the body seems to have been laid out, in fact it has been laid out, on his back, arms by his side, legs together, something that you can only do with a fresh corpse.'

'He could have been killed here, in fact,' Sussock suggested.

'He could have been,' Reynolds conceded. 'It's a distinct possibility. I'll trawl for indications of the probable locus in the lab. Do you know when it started raining tonight? The Meteorological Office will be able to tell us exactly.' Reynolds knelt. 'No, it doesn't matter,' he said, feeling the ground underneath the body, 'the ground under him is as soaked as anywhere and everywhere else. It had occurred to me that if the ground, the area of rubble he covered, was dry and we knew when the rain started we might have some indication of when he was brought here.' Reynolds stood and slapped grit and mud from his palms. 'But that clue is not available to us. All I can say is that he was brought after it started raining. Excuse my rambling, Sergeant. Do you know him, incidentally?'

Sussock shook his head. 'We haven't been able to identify him, sir.'

'Well-dressed man,' said Reynolds. 'Have you been through his pockets? No wallet, cheque-book?'

'Haven't touched anything yet, sir.'

'I see.' Reynolds stooped to pick up his bag. 'Well, I can't really do anything else here. I'll make my way to the infirmary if you'd care to bring him down. Separate body bag for the head, please.'

'Of course, sir. We've only got the photographs to take, and if our forensic chemist could lift the fingerprints at the laboratory – when you have completed the post-mortem, of course . . .'

'Certainly. No problem at all.' Reynolds turned and walked towards his Volvo which he had parked behind the mortuary van. He was a tall, silver-haired man and Sussock thought he made a striking, if not eerie, figure as he strode across the rubble, walking between the two bands of tape, holding a multi-coloured golfing umbrella above his head in the gathering dawn light, a light continually pierced by three blue revolving lights. Reynolds got into his Volvo in a calm, unhurried manner and drove away down Maryhill Road. Just another man doing just another job.

She came off the towpath and walked down the embankment and between the factory units. She saw one car, a police car, one of the small ones just cruising by. She watched it go. She took a last look around, she couldn't see them and she had to be home for her man. She walked across Garscube Road, awash with rainwater, and entered her close in the new low-rise development. She tried her door. It was shut. She banged on it. Soon an arm reached over her shoulder and unlocked the door. Inside the flat she began to feel warm and was dimly aware of gentle hands peeling sodden clothing away from her shoulders.

Reynolds opened the smaller bag first. It was made of the same heavy duty plastic as the large body bag, and was of the type usually employed to carry severed limbs from the scene of road accidents, or the bodies of newborn infants which are found with saddening frequency in the city's dustbins and back courts, occasionally in the scheme streets, left lying where they dropped. On this occasion the bag contained a head which Reynolds lifted with both hands and placed on the dissecting table. The hair of the severed head was still neatly slicked in place and the eyes were open and they seemed to stare at Sussock, who stood deferentially in the corner of the pathology laboratory. The third person in the room was the mortuary attendant, a small man with greased-down hair whose lips were also small and tight, but who always wore a sinister smile in his eyes – a look which never failed to unnerve Sussock. Reynolds then unzipped the top of the larger body bag and hooked his hands under the arms of the corpse and held them there while the attendant pulled the bag away.

'So,' said Reynolds, switching on the tape-recorder which he carried in the pocket of his laboratory coat, and speaking into the small microphone attached to the lapel. 'Here we go.' Then he matter-of-factly recorded the date, April 1st. 'Hope this isn't a lark, Sergeant.'

'No, sir,' said Sussock who had hoped for the last two hours that no one would succumb to making the remark that Reynolds had just made. 'Hardly, sir. Hardly a joke.'

'Well, to continue, a male Caucasian of unknown identity, head severed completely from the body by one major blow from behind and the separation completed with a series of blows with a sharp instrument.'

'A cleaver?' said Sussock suddenly.

Reynolds switched off the tape-recorder and nodded to Sussock – 'That sort of thing – ' and then switched the tape-recorder on again. 'Eyes open, indicating that the victim was conscious at the time of death, there is no apparent injury to the head other than the damage to the vertebrae and the neck and throat tissue.' He switched off the tape-recorder and turned to the assistant. 'If you'll help me, please?' Together they removed the man's clothing, item by item, and placed each garment, no matter how small, into a separate Cellophane bag. When the man was completely naked the attendant draped a towel over the man's middle, or, as is officially termed, his 'private parts'.

'I'll have the clothing sent over to the Forensic Science Lab,' Reynolds said to Sussock. 'Would you like to check the pockets now or later?'

'Now, please,' said Sussock. He took the clothing and laid the Cellophane bag on the table at the side of the pathology laboratory, opened each bag and felt in the pockets. In fact there were only two garments he could examine, the jacket and the trousers. He felt in the pockets of each and then shook his head.

'Oh, bad luck,' said Reynolds and turned to the corpse. He switched on the tape-recorder. 'There is no other indication of injury. I will test for poisoning later, but my initial finding is that the cause of death in this case was a sudden and unexpected blow to the back of the neck just above the first vertebra with a sharp edge which severed the head almost but not quite completely from the body. This first and fatal blow was followed up with a series of further blows from a sharp-edged weapon by which the head was completely separated from the trunk. I estimate that death occurred sometime between 10.00 P.M. and midnight yesterday, given that he was left clothed, under a sheet, out of doors when the temperature was approximately three degrees Celsius.' Reynolds switched off the tape-recorder. 'Well, that's as far as I can go, Sergeant, not particularly helpful, I'm afraid. His hair is his own, and not dyed, he kept himself very clean, no grease or muck under the finger-nails which could have told us something about him. Forensic Science might be able to tell you more.'

'Well, at least we have something to work on, a time of death. Can we ask our forensic assistant to attend here and lift the fingerprints?'

'Certainly. I don't think we are booked this morning.' Reynolds glanced at the assistant who shook his head.

'I'll phone him now, sir. Can I use the phone in your office?'

'Please do, Sergeant.'

Elliot Bothwell was thirty-six years of age and he lived with his mother in Queen's Park. He was overweight, awkward in movement and for the last fifteen years he had thought that maybe next year he would not be feeling so gauche, he might even develop a sense of dress. Each night he would be in bed by ten-thirty with a cup of cocoa on the cabinet next to his bed, he'd lie back with his hands clasped behind his head and wonder how to go about developing an image, how to cut a dash. Occasionally he had attempted to put ideas into practice and the result was always embarrassing, often spectacularly so. He always thought he ought never to have bought the trendy kaftan coat, for example. As he lay there each night his ideas about how to cut a dash were gradually dislodged as memories of embarrassing, guilt-inducing incidents in his past, memories which he had managed to suppress during the day, resurfaced. These memories would push themselves to the front of his mind, each one as clear and fresh as on the day he had perpetrated the social gaffe in question. On some nights he would have to relive his entire catalogue of awkward moments, on others a single awful incident would be relived over and over again. It was during this phase that he would slowly turn on to one side and curl into the foetal posture in which he slept and in which he usually awoke. And usually he woke to find that he had not drunk his cocoa and it stood, cold, with a surface skin, where he had placed it on his bedside table.

Elliot Bothwell had started his working life as a chemistry assistant in an inner city secondary school, which was grandly called an Academy. He spent ten years mixing the same calm chemicals in a small room behind the classroom in which, Bothwell observed, the teacher turned grey as he tried to teach chemistry to class after class while the pupils throughout those ten years were more interested in refining the technique of exploding test tubes in Bunsen burner flames. Then he noticed a vacancy for the post of Forensic Assistant with the Strathclyde Police, based at the P Division Police Station at Charing Cross. He got the job and never looked back. It paid an enchanced rate for 'unsocial hours' and a little extra as 'call-out money'. 'Call-out money' was received as an automatic component in his monthly salary, but was only occasionally earned. The early hours of the morning of April 1st were just such an occasion.

The phone by his bed rang with a harsh rattling tone, insistent and penetrating, ending only when he succeeded in knocking it off the cabinet on to the floor as he groped for it while uncurling from the foetal position in which he slept. He moved his hand across the carpet, found the cord and pulled until he held the receiver. He drew the receiver under the sheets and said, 'Bothwell,' then he listened and said, 'Yes, I'll be right there.'

He rose from his bed, clumsily, shaking off sleep. He glanced at his watch, 04.40. Outside the cats in the backs were howling and screaming like babies. He dressed with quick, jerky movements and with an untidy result. Then he undressed, washed, and dressed again, this time slightly tidier, having been refreshed with cold water and toothpaste. The floorboards in the hall creaked as he walked on them and his mother wailed from her room, 'Elliot, the cats, see to the cats, Elliot.'

He left the flat and walked down the chill stone common stairway, the stairlight throwing long shadows as he passed. In the backs the cats sat on the fence and the walls and looked at him curiously. He said 'Shoo!' and waved his arms. The cats just sat and looked at him.

Elliot Bothwell had never seen a headless corpse before and he stood and stared at the spectacle. He had seen dead bodies before in all states of dress and all states of decomposition, but never one like this, lying there on the stainless steel table, with the towel, as is usual, over the middle and the head one foot away from the body, laid on its side mercifully, perhaps intentionally, sensitively facing away from the door of the post-mortem laboratory. Also in the room were Detective-Sergeant Sussock and the mortuary assistant. Both stood at the edge of the room and noticeably distant from each other. Elliot Bothwell wore thick-lensed spectacles, he moved clumsily and much escaped him, but even he, never blessed with great insight, saw plainly that Sussock and the mortuary assistant disliked each other.

'It's what happens when a man loses his head,' said the mortuary assistant, and he seemed to Bothwell to be more keen to eclipse Sussock than he was to strike up a conversation with the forensic chemist. 'He gets the chop.'

Ray Sussock had never known the mortuary assistant to speak when Dr Reynolds was present, unless it was to reply to a specific question. The small man with greased-down hair and sinister gleam in his eyes merely went about his job with hurried efficiency. It was only when Dr Reynolds had left the laboratory that the assistant's personality emerged and when it did it did not surprise Sussock, it just confirmed what he had long suspected lay behind those eyes; an unpleasant sense of humour.

'Snicker snack,' said Bothwell, and laid his case on the stainless steel table.

Ray Sussock had once known another mortuary assistant. It was in the old days, the halcyon days of youthful and happy marriage with an infant son, the days before they bought the bungalow, after which things had begun to go wrong. The other mortuary assistant had been a neighbour across the stair when they stayed in the tenement. This man had worked as he said 'all my days' in the mortuary and when Sussock met him he was elderly, close to his retirement, and he knew exactly what was to happen to his body should there be any suspicion or unknown cause about his death. He knew who would hold which instrument, which would be placed here and drawn down to here, and then here to here, and here to here, to expose his chest with three neat incisions enabling the flesh to be peeled back like petals of a flower. Or, if he collapsed suddenly, which blade would be run around his head enabling the scalp to be pulled down over his face, which small electric circular-saw would be used to cut his skull neatly in two on a horizontal axis, like a hard boiled egg being sliced in two, so that the top part could be lifted off and his brain removed. This man knew all this and feared his own death more than Sussock had known or was ever to know. He would come home each evening and stay in his flat until he had to leave for work the next morning. On one occasion he had to go out in the evening to a social function, and Sussock clearly remembered how his wife coaxed him down the stair: 'There, it's all right, just one at a time, the taxi's waiting, no, it won't crash, of course it won't crash, now the turn of the stair, here we go . . .' Sussock wondered if the mortuary assistant in the room that April morning would become like that. Perhaps he already was like that and the apparent necrophilia and black humour was just an elaborate defence. God knows, he couldn't do this man's job and if he had to do it then he too would need something to help him get through the working day.

Bothwell took an ink-soaked pad and pressed each of the dead man's fingertips on to the pad, then he pressed each of the fingerprints in turn on to the appropriate square on a sheet of thick but fine-grained paper, each square marked index finger to thumb, left hand and right hand, one sheet of paper for each hand. This done he slipped each sheet of paper into a wallet of clear Cellophane.

'Anything else, Mr Sussock?'

Sussock shook his head. 'The clothing has already gone off to the Forensic Laboratory, we're just waiting for the fingerprints.'

'I'll have them processed immediately, Mr Sussock. I should be able to get the results to you in an hour if he's known locally, but the Police National Computer at Hendon won't come back until later today, mid-afternoon at the earliest, really depends on the availability of computer time.'

'Good enough.' Sussock walked to the door, pleased to leave the mortuary assistant to finish up. Pleased to leave the presence of the mortuary assistant, pleased to leave the hospital.

Elliot Bothwell followed Sussock down the wide warm corridor in the humming basement bowels of the infirmary, dull yellow tiles, green painted pipes running along the ceiling. He passed a door with a red sign which read 'Danger Radioactive', and he thought it was some job he had, fingerprinting a headless corpse at five-thirty in the morning. Still, it was better than watching the chemistry teacher turn grey.

Phil Hamilton was just finishing the night shift at 05.30, walking at faster than normal pace along Great Western Road towards St George's to turn right towards Charing Cross, reporting in, writing up, signing off, a mug of coffee, and home. After leaving the gap site in Maryhill he'd continued his beat and watched the city wake. First it was the milk boys, isolated figures who had pulled themselves out of their pits and were crossing the city in singles or in pairs, sometimes in small groups, making for the dairies. Then it was the vans and milk-floats rattling in the streets and those same milk boys running to and from their vehicles, delivering the milk at double time, often inconsiderately shouting to each other and so prematurely waking citizens still slumbering in their flats. Then the first buses, apart from the all-night services, which ran empty out of the city to the outlying towns or schemes, the vans dropping bundles of newspapers outside newsagents' shops. These last he kept an eye on; some wide boys made a good living following the delivery vans and picking up the newspapers and trucking them elsewhere for re-sale. Hamilton stopped off at a newsagent just as the proprietor, an Indian, was hacking at the twine which bound the copies of the early edition of the *Glasgow Herald.* Hamilton bought a packet of nails and resumed his walk to P Division Police Station. Curiously, he thought, the impression he would take home with him wasn't the dead man with the severed head, or the figure hurrying along the towpath, it was the time that the birds began to kick up their din. It wasn't a dawn chorus at all, it started at three A.M., maybe four, but certainly a good two hours before the sky cracked.

When the birds started to sing he found the sound enjoyable. So he smoked a cigarette and listened to them. On this occasion he smoked it openly, thinking it unwise to find a secluded place.

Chapter Two

April 1st, 09.15 hours.

Donoghue read Sussock's report and then he read Hamilton's report. Then he poured a second mug of coffee from the tall chrome coffee-pot and read the reports again. Sussock, sitting patiently, silently in front of Donoghue's desk sighed as he watched Donghue turn again to the beginning of the reports. Donoghue sensed Sussock's impatience, but this was police work, and they were alive and could indulge in impatience. Impatience, Donoghue felt, was a luxury which had been suddenly denied to the man whose body had been found on a gap site in Maryhill. As a major concession to the older man, who had just finished a night shift, Donoghue said, 'Another coffee, Ray?'

The older man forced his eyelids up a little and said, 'No thank you, sir.'

Donoghue wasn't really listening. Sussock watched him, the Detective-Inspector, in at eight-thirty a.m. sharp, coming all the way from Edinburgh in his Rover, rain or snow, winter time, summer time, heavy traffic or clear roads, he'd be in at eight-thirty sharp, five days a week. Seven if necessary. Smartly dressed, always in a three-piece suit, always with a gold hunter's chain looped across his waistcoat front. Slowly, without taking his eyes off the report, Donoghue reached for his pipe with its slightly curved stem, put it in his mouth and lit the tobacco with his gold-plated lighter. Then he grunted and Sussock sat forward, knowing that Donoghue was about to, as he was fond of saying, 'kick the matter about'.

'So let's kick it about, Ray,' he said, pulling on his pipe.

Ray Sussock shuffled in his chair. 'Yes, sir,' he managed, and wondered how old Donoghue was. Forty, forty-two, he thought.

'So we have a man murdered on our patch, definitely murdered, attacked from the rear with a razor-sharp cleaver which killed him outright, opened his eyes that did, I dare say, he was murdered in a locus as yet unknown and his body carried to the place where it was found by PC Hamilton.'

'Yes, sir.'

'What was Hamilton doing on the waste ground in a rainstorm? Having a smoke?'

'Most probably, sir,' said Sussock. 'His breath smelled of cigarette smoke when we spoke.'

'Have a word with him, Ray.'

Sussock grunted.

'The initial post-mortem report indicated that death was due to the obvious, that is, the severing of the head from the body. There is no indication of other damage, accidental or otherwise. Fingerprints . . . ?'

'Bothwell handed them to the collator, nothing on

our files. They were then sent down the wire to Hendon, no feedback yet, bit early in the piece to expect it, right enough.'

'Probably overloaded.' Donoghue sucked and blew on his pipe. 'It's probably been a busy weekend up and down the Kingdom and we'll just have to take our place in the queue. Clothing?'

'Already sent off to the Forensic Laboratory, sir.' Sussock glanced at his watch. 'I dare say that allowing for morning coffee to get their brains into gear, the scientists will be beginning work on them about now. We could expect feedback on the clothes by midday.'

'At the latest I would hope, Ray. At the latest. I take it we don't know him from missing persons or mug shots of locally cultivated felons?'

'I . . .'

'We did photograph the head, I trust, particularly the face?'

'It . . . you see, sir, there was . . .'

'Well, get a scene of crimes officer down to the Royal Infirmary to photograph the head as soon as you like, Ray. Who's on the day shift in CID?'

'Abernethy, sir.'

'Good enough. Ask him to try and identify the photograph of the deceased, please. If he concentrates on the volumes of the – what would you say, Ray? Twenty-five to forty-year-olds, no, make that up to fifty-year-olds – that should give us a wide enough margin. Ought not to be more than fourteen volumes, it'll keep him occupied for an hour or two. He does have room for this, I take it?'

'Do any of us?' It wasn't a facetious reply.

'No, I daresay we don't. What's he got on at the moment?'

'Burglaries, one aggravated, a wilful fire-raising which could be linked to other similar fire-raising incidents, usual gamut of car thefts, a few petty neds caught in possession of heroin who won't tell us the names of their supplier.'

'Nor would I in their circumstances,' said Donoghue. 'Once you grass on the drug business you're not safe anywhere, even in the slammer.'

'One or two other cases as well sir, but that's all I can recall. His filing cabinet drawer is bulging as much as anybody's.'

'Well, I think he can give this some priority. My feelings are that this could be something sinister. You see, he was well dressed so if this is rough justice of the kind beloved in the underworld, then he was probably up to his oxters in something heavy.'

'Not a petty ned you mean, sir.'

'Exactly.'

'Now the murder itself, very lucky, very, very lucky, or very, very skilful.'

'Everything else is so neat, sir. Skill would seem more likely than luck.'

'I think so too, Ray. The way he seems to have been carried from the locus of the offence and then his body laid out under a sheet with his head sitting on the chest . . . well, it seems to have been planned very carefully. Did we sweep the ground?'

'Yes, sir, as soon as daylight permitted. Nothing

of apparent note. The rain prevented us from taking plaster casts, difficult anyway, mainly rubble with very few areas of soil. We've still got two constables there at the moment keeping the public off the area.'

'Good, we may well want to go back when and if we ever know what we are looking for.'

'Indeed, sir.'

'So a professional topping. Deceased's personal effects removed to hinder identification. He was well dressed, and that could indicate organized crime.'

'Certainly could, sir.' Sussock shook his head in an attempt to fight off sleep, but the sense of fatigue came flooding back within seconds.

'You know what suggests that this is perhaps not a professional job?'

'Sir?'

'Well, I'm just kicking it about but, well, think, Ray. What's the argument against this being the work of organized crime?'

'Can't think.' It was a very truthful answer. He didn't care if his testiness showed. He glanced at the metal upright cabinet behind Donoghue's desk, it had a grey frame but the door had been painted blue. The blue and the grey merged together as his eyes swam. He concentrated his focus and the door and frame once again became distinct.

'What do you think about the way the body was left in the open, on a piece of waste ground close to the point where two arterial roads meet?'

But Sussock remained silent.

'When in the past we have come across the results

of organized crime meting out its own justice, it's only messy if they are pushed for time or if they're disturbed. If they can take their time they go to great lengths to hide the body. When a decomposed body is discovered in a remote part of Scotland, it's as often as not eventually identified as the corpse of a known crook who disappeared from the streets of London some years previously. We have still to identify the headless, limbless corpse which was washed up on the banks of the Clyde some years ago, and when we do, I've a month's salary that says it's the result of an underworld execution, and not necessarily the Glasgow underworld. There's the flyover near the centre of the city which always seems to need resurfacing, and I think there's more than a grain of truth in the explanation that the surface is cracking due to unsound foundations; too many dead bodies in the concrete, so they say.'

'I see.' But Sussock didn't. The blue and the grey were once again beginning to merge.

'Too neat for a fight that went too far. Too "loud" to be the underworld. The boy who pulled this stunt is twisted, a State Hospital number. It's the sort of case that makes our job difficult.'

In his office, smaller, colder, and more spartan than Donoghue's, Sussock stood wearily in his old Gannex coat and battered trilby, and reached for his phone. He dialled a two-figure number. 'Scene of crimes?' he said when his call was answered. 'Yes, I'd like . . .' and he relayed Donoghue's request for photographs of the head of the deceased to be taken.

He went down the CID corridor and spoke to Abernethy, advising him of the photographs which would be coming his way later in the day. 'If you could identify him, please,' he said, 'either missing persons or known offenders.'

'Very good, Sarge.' Abernethy nodded. Alert, enthusiastic. Then Sussock drove home, thankfully.

Home. Once it must have been a magnificent house. Once it was the dwelling for the family of a merchant banker, or a shipping magnate or a tobacco lord, with the servants living on the ground floor behind the heavily barred windows, the bars being designed to keep the servants in, not burglars out. Now it was a crumbling building of uncertain future. A similar building two doors down had already been demolished because it was an unsound structure, the building on the other side of the street, of similar vintage, was unashamedly fronted with massive timber shorings. The house stood in the bohemian West End of Glasgow, and Detective-Sergeant Raymond Sussock, at the age of fifty-five, rented a bedsit on the first floor. He shared a kitchen which was one flight of stairs below his room. That morning he went to the kitchen immediately upon entering the house, feeling the need for a cup of tea, and found, not really to his surprise, that his food store had been plundered. The cheese had been attacked, brazenly, not even with a knife, but somebody, Sussock noted with a professional eye, with a missing top incisor had taken a bite out of it. The recently opened packet of tea-bags had been reduced to two bags and Sussock had the impression that it was only out of charity on the part of the thief that even these remained. Sussock tore the tea-bags apart, put one in the small teapot and put the kettle on the gas.

It was still reasonably early for the house, not yet ten A.M., and the building was silent. There is a rule, golden and unbendable, laid down by the Scottish Office, that a serving police officer cannot live in the same household as a person who has been convicted of a criminal offence, which is why Sussock's early years, as a constable and a single man, were spent living in a succession of 'approved lodgings', all run by militaristic matriarchs, or in the police dwellings with no less comfortable regimes. His present accommodation was strictly temporary and it was because of his years of service and rank that the police force had not checked on his address with the alacrity that it would have done had he been a fresh-faced constable. It was a 'dodgy' house with the gruntings of homosexual matings penetrating the thin walls, with Mad Max in the next room who was so petrified of the Martian invasion that the tall, soft-spoken man with 'Psycho Billy' tattooed on his arm would give Mad Max a plastic toy pistol. Mad Max would then sit on the edge of his bed waiting for the Martians until he fell asleep, whereupon Psycho Billy would tiptoe into his room to retrieve the pistol until it was needed again. There were the odd shifty-eyed people whom Sussock passed on the stair, there was the ringing of the doorbell at three A.M. as if in code, two short, pause, one long, and then two more short rings followed by hushed conversation in the hall.

Sussock would have been the first to concede that

his accommodation would not meet with the approval of the Chief Constable, and would readily agree that he was 'pushing it a bit' and if pressed would admit to 'pushing it a lot'. So far he had got away with it. It was, he kept telling himself, strictly temporary, but he found himself sitting in the only armchair looking out of the window and watching the seasons change. He took the tea up to his room and sat in the chair holding the mug in both hands. He looked around, the unmade bed, his trousers hanging over the heater. He didn't want to sleep in this room, or more accurately he didn't want to wake up in the room. He washed and changed his shirt. He went downstairs, out into the rain, into his car and drove to the other side of the water, to Langside.

Foreign, thought Abernethy, as he studied the five-by-nine-inch black and white photographs of the face of the dead man, full frontal, full profile, half profile, still tacky from the developing tank, and still smelling of the sickly sweet aroma of the developing chemicals. Abernethy held the full frontal photograph at arm's length and studied it. He thought that the dead man had been blessed with a well-balanced face, if a little on the lean side; he had rich waxy hair and a pencil-line moustache and was otherwise clean-shaven, although the photographs showed after-death growth of whiskers. The deceased's nose was straight and like his face, thin, but by no means extremely so. Had he been vain, Abernethy brooded, this man would probably have considered himself beautiful, not having the ruggedness to be handsome. The man's ears were pressed close to his head, not noticeably so, it was only under closer scrutiny that they seemed a little more flat against the skull than was normal. The eyes stared at Abernethy with the unmistakable look of shock frozen on them, but underneath the look of sudden horror they seemed to be full, they seemed to be the eyes of a man who gave and received emotional warmth, even if tainted with a degree of narcissism. Abernethy felt a certain cynicism towards the man, being awkward at the age of twenty-one and still suffering traces of residual acne. None the less, the overall impression, for no reason he could put his finger on, was that the dead man was a foreigner. He was a Caucasian, like most men in Glasgow; there are handsome men in Glasgow, there are thin-faced men, there are men with thick waxy hair, there are men with moustaches, yet for some reason as he studied the photographs the phrase 'not of this town' came to Abernethy's mind again and again. He pinned the photograph to the board mounted on the wall beside his desk, pushed his mug of coffee to one side and reached for the first volume of photographs of known criminals in Glasgow and the environs, six photographs to a page listed by date of birth and coded by number, in order to maintain a certain confidentiality on the occasions when a member of the public is asked to cooperate by glancing over the volumes. Each volume was three inches thick, and he had fifteen volumes lying on his desk which he had signed out of Criminal Records. Beyond those volumes lay another six volumes labelled Missing Persons. Detective-Constable Abernethy began to leaf carefully through the volumes of photographs at two minutes past ten A.M. on the morning of Monday, 1st April. Two and three-quarter hours later his feeling that the deceased was 'not of this town' was confirmed. At least it was strengthened. The man was not a known criminal, nor had he been reported as missing. Abernethy wrote a brief memorandum to Donoghue indicating the result, or lack thereof, of his screening of the photographs. He slipped the memorandum into Donoghue's pigeonhole at the top end of the CID corridor and went to the canteen for a late lunch.

Jean Kay was a small grey-haired woman in her fifties. She moved with small hurried movements, quick and, to her youthful and plump assistant, annoyingly efficient. She held a top second science degree and a good doctorate, and she spent her working life as a Forensic Scientist employed by the Scottish Office. Her present place of employment was the modern, newly built Forensic Science Laboratory in Pitt Street. She worked mainly with the Strathclyde Police, but was indeed pleased to be called upon to provide a service to the Police Forces of the Grampians, Tayside, Central, Highlands and Islands and, occasionally, from the more professionally competitive Lothian and Borders Police. Such was the reputation of the modern, newly built laboratory in Pitt Street where she worked.

The items of clothing which were last worn by the man who was found in Maryhill earlier that morning had arrived at the laboratory in plastic sachets of varying size, one garment in each sachet, as had the scrapings from the dead man's fingernails.

The jacket first, eased carefully out of the plastic bag and laid on the bench. A great deal of modern technology was available to Jean Kay, but she began the meticulous survey of the jacket by an honest to God inspection with hand and naked eye. She noticed that the jacket was clean. It was noticeably free of surface grime and grit, though traces of grease lay deep within the weave. Similarly the edges of the sleeves were worn and the lining at the wrists had been darkened. It was the first finding of crucial importance. Jean Kay did not need an electron microscope or infra-red photography to inform her that the jacket had been recently drycleaned. She turned the collar back and swept the crease for debris. A few fibres, a piece of darkened grit, seemed to have escaped the drycleaner, and these she gathered carefully and placed in a small self-sealing Cellophane sachet which she then handed to her assistant for labelling. She then noted each stage of the scientific investigation in her notebook.

In much the same way that the young and inexperienced Detective-Constable Abernethy had found the word 'foreign' pushing itself to the forefront of his mind as he studied the pasty features of the dead man, the word 'clean' kept re-occurring to the highly experienced Jean Kay as she trawled carefully through the deceased's clothing. It was clean in the hygienic sense of the word, in fact it was more than clean following laundering, 'sanitized', in a word, it was a cleanness which came only with newness. Some items, even the shirt and socks felt used and even smelled very slightly, but nevertheless still smelled new. She subjected the underpants to microscopic scrutiny, searching for semen or urine deposits. There were none. The man's underpants were undoubtedly recently purchased, as were his socks, shirt and tie. Jean Kay took the man's shoes from the plastic bag and was not surprised to find that these too were new. It is not necessary to be a scientist of many years' experience to tell that shoes which appear to be modern in design, are not worn away at the sole or heel or scuffed on the toe, and shine if the grime is wiped away, are new. Especially if they smell new.

'They're new,' she said to her assistant, as she sniffed at the shoes.

Within half an hour Jean Kay was certain that she was not examining the dead man's clothes so much as she was examining the clothes worn by the man when his corpse was found. That was the only certain thing that she could assume. She could not even assume that the clothes were worn by the man at the moment of his death.

She left the bench and crossed to a desk which stood in the corner of the laboratory. She took the report from the folder which had accompanied the clothes from the pathology laboratory of the Glasgow Royal Infirmary, and read again that death had been due to decapitation with a sharp-edged weapon striking the rear of the deceased's neck. Jean Kay re-crossed the laboratory to the workbench, took up her pen with a flourish, which her assistant had long ago recognized as an indication of shortness of temper, and wrote in her notebook.

1) All clothing new except the suit which has been recently drycleaned. New clothes bought or at least unwrapped a matter of hours before being worn by the deceased.
2) Clothing placed on body *after* death. There is not the slightest trace of blood on any garment.

Given the sinister cleanliness of the clothing, it was with an almost perfunctory attitude that she began to turn out the pockets of the suit. The jacket and trousers revealed nothing; a waistcoat pocket contained gold dust. She extracted it with her fingers and, despite the delicacy of her touch, the item began to crumble. She laid it on the bench. It was paper, printed paper, about four inches square when unfolded. It seemed to have been inadvertently wedged into the waistcoat pocket and forgotten. On the top of the paper was faded printing, but Jean Kay could clearly make out the heading: Ardmore Hotel, Saltcoats. Underneath were three lines of writing in ballpoint, written in a round loopy hand, most probably, thought the scientist, by a female. She could make out the word 'received' and that the amount was a double figure next to a pound sterling sign and zero pence. It was a receipt from the Ardmore Hotel for a round figure in excess of

£10.00, but less than £100.00. She took the flimsy piece of paper and slid it between two sheets of Cellophane and handed it to her assistant, who took hold of it gingerly. 'Photomagnification, please,' she said. 'Factor of five ought to do it.'

The man sat in his office, relaxing in his chair, pulling gently on his pipe, enjoying the taste of the tobacco, a special mix he had made up for him by a city tobacconist, it had a Dutch base for taste and a twist of dark shag for depth of flavour and for a slower burning rate. Occasionally he glanced outside his window up the length of Sauchiehall Street, the queues of buses of half a dozen different companies which was the result of the free-for-all following the deregulation of the bus routes. The buses were brightly coloured: the grubby orange buses of the Transport Executive, the always bristlingly clean, bright blue and yellow buses of the Kelvin Scottish, the red and orange vehicles of the Clydeside Scottish bus company, and the lightly named but certainly highly efficient 'Magic Bus' company vehicles. They were all bumper to bumper with taxis and private cars, the people on the pavement scurrying in the rain, or walking slowly, resignedly with hunched shoulders, the down-and-outs picking through the yellow rubbish bins which were fastened to the street lamp-posts. He turned from the window and considered the ceiling, beginning again to stain brown with nicotine. He pulled and blew on his pipe. He had only himself to blame, but he made a mental note to mention it to the cleaners. The man was not displeased with his morning's work. He had something of substance to discuss with the Chief Inspector. He had a murder file already bulging with submissions and photographs, he had an inquiry which was still less than twelve hours old. The reports indicated a violent death, certainly murder, curiously clean clothing, a possible link with a hotel in Saltcoats. It was enough to be going on with for the time being. Beside the file was a master copy of a poster which showed the man's face, frontal and profile, with the caption 'Do You Know This Man?', a small paragraph about the date and place his body was found, and the request that any member of the public who thought he or she could give evidence should telephone P Division Police Station, Charing Cross, Glasgow, 'or any police station'. He would need the Chief Inspector's approval before he could ask for the poster to be duplicated and distributed to other police stations and public places, such as bus and railway stations and city centre pubs. He poured himself a coffee. The inquiry was beginning to gather momentum and he was aware of the need to continue that momentum. If momentum flags, morale flags, individual officers lose interest, public criticism grows.

The phone on the man's desk rang. He placed his pipe in the huge black ashtray which he kept on his desk and about which a junior officer had once said, 'All you need is some tap water and a couple of goldfish now, sir,' and reached forward for the phone. He picked it up and said, 'Detective-Inspector Donoghue.'

'Reynolds here,' said a soft-spoken male voice at the other end of the line. 'Glasgow Royal Infirmary, pathology.'

'Yes, sir,' said Donoghue, instinctively reaching for his pad and ballpoint.

'I've just completed my examination of the deceased, that is to say the headless corpse who was brought in this morning . . .'

'Yes, sir.' Donoghue wedged the telephone between his ear and shoulder and held the pad with one hand while he wrote with the other.

'I've a little more information for you,' continued Reynolds. 'The cause of death is as previously thought, that is decapitation, there is no indication of poisoning or death from natural causes, such as heart failure, cerebral haemorrhage, or some such.'

'His head was chopped off,' said Donoghue.

'Yes, in a word,' said Reynolds. 'There was a slight trace of barbiturates in the blood, but no more than would be the case if the deceased had been prescribed a mild course of sleeping pills, and had been taking such pills for a number of years.'

'I see, sir.' Donoghue scribbled.

'Of interest is that his body was cleaned. There is no trace of blood anywhere on the surface of his body.'

'Dr Kay, our Forensic Scientist, has also made a similar observation, sir. There is apparently no blood on his clothing, and even more curious is that the clothing itself seems to have been new, with the exception of the suit, which had been recently drycleaned, but even so all clothing seems to have been placed on the deceased after death. He was not wearing the clothes in which he was found at the moment of his death.'

'Well, that would fit with my finding that the body has been washed, probably with industrial alcohol. There's hardly a trace of grime in the pores. It's normal procedure that corpses are washed, in this case it's as though it has been done for us. The lack of blood on the clothing is interesting. It's a significant point which I missed myself, it's alarming how easy it is for the obvious to escape one's notice. In a death of this nature there would have been a massive amount of blood spilled.'

'There would?'

'Oh, indeed. You see, if I were to come up behind you when you were not expecting me, and if I had a sharp enough weapon which could take your head off in one swing, and I did that, then the next pump of your heart would send a geyser of blood fifteen feet into the air.'

'That doesn't bear thinking about.'

'It's significant, though, because the locus of this offence will have been left in a very bloody mess.'

'Unless it was cleaned up like the corpse appears to have been.'

'Well, that's your department, Inspector. My report will be following in due course, probably towards the end of the day, or early tomorrow morning.'

'Thank you, sir,' said Donoghue, ready to put the phone down. But Reynolds had not finished.

'I've paid a little more attention to the age of the corpse.'

'Oh?'

'I think I can narrow it down to being the corpse of a man in his forties, nothing scientific about the process, just looking at the face and imagining life and movement being present. I think he lived well but healthily.'

'Lived well?'

'Well, he wasn't a manual labourer, his fingers and palms are soft and fleshy, he never picked up anything heavier than a pen in the course of his working day. I opened his stomach and spent an hour or so doing some detective work. There were the remains of a meal, probably eaten an hour or two before he was slain. The contents were gelatinous in texture, some rice, partially masticated white meat, some vegetable matter which turned out to be chestnuts and some stringy stuff that had me foxed for a while and which turned out to be bamboo shoots.'

'A meal in a Chinese restaurant,' said Donoghue.

Reynolds paused. 'You stole my punchline,' he groaned.

Donoghue smiled. It was not often that he scored a point off the respected pathologist.

'In very good health generally,' continued the pathologist drily. 'A teetotaller, I would suspect. Men in their forties, especially those who frequent restaurants, usually show some deterioration in their kidneys and liver due to alcohol. In some cases they are shot to hell already. In this man's case, they are as clean as a whistle. It's a shame he didn't have a kidney donor card on his person, we could have used these organs.'

'A clean-living man, but a good-living man,' Donoghue scribbled on his notepad.

'Yes.' Reynolds still sounded angry. 'His teeth, always a mine of information about a person. I shall be taking casts rather than amputating the jaw.'

'I'd prefer you didn't amputate,' Donoghue cut in with a sense of alarm. 'We might still have to ask the next of kin to identify the body. It'll be difficult enough for them as it is.'

'Very well. I shall send the casts to the School of Dentistry, they might be able to match them against records. He certainly has been no stranger to dental treatment. He has a large number of fillings and there is the beginning of cavities between the teeth and the gum, which indicates gum disease. It's at the stage where the teeth were beginning to loosen. The cavities are clear and so I guessed that he had recently, and I mean within the last seven days, received the attention of a dental hygienist who cleared away the plaque deposits and gave him a strong warning about the life-expectancy of his teeth, because there is indication of diligent tooth-brushing following the removal of the plaque.'

'I see.' Donoghue continued to scribble.

'I can tell the treatment from the dental hygienist was recent because, as well as the evident cleanliness, there are still small slivers of plaque in the back crevices of his mouth, which have been dislodged from the teeth and gum but have not been taken away by the suction pipe or the mouthwash. Not doing any harm at all, but indicating very recent treatment. In a few days they would have been caught up in the food and swallowed harmlessly into the stomach.'

'Within seven days.'

'At the extreme outside. That's just me covering myself. Off the record I'd say three days was a better bet. Today's Monday, dentists like to work a five-day week.'

'Indicating treatment on Friday last?'

'That sort of thing,' said Reynolds.

'I'd go for Friday,' said Donoghue.

'So would I.' Reynolds seemed to be warming again. 'But I'm encroaching on your territory yet again.'

'Oh, encroach as much as you like, sir.' Donoghue sat forward as he grasped the opportunity to prevent their conversation being terminated while there was still the slightest trace of ill-feeling between them.

'Even if the dentist in question has a Saturday surgery, then it will most likely be full of schoolchildren or chaps who can't get time off mid-week. The deceased seems to be the sort of man who can organize his own time within reason.'

'So the deceased had an appointment with the dental hygienist three days ago.'

'It's a most reasonable assumption, Inspector. Good day.'

'Good day and thank you, sir.' Donoghue replaced the phone gently.

He glanced at the clock on his wall. Two P.M.

Time for a stroll to the water and back. He had a meeting with Chief Inspector Findlater at three. He picked up the phone again and dialled a two-figure internal number.

'Abernethy,' said the crisp voice on the other end of the line.

'DI Donoghue,' said Donoghue.

'Yes, sir.'

'I've just read your report, Abernethy. Just a word about your choice of expression. I think "not of this town" is a trifle flowery, a little poetic, don't you? In future a simple transmission of information or opinion will suffice.'

'Yes, sir. I'll bear that in mind.'

But as each man replaced his telephone receiver, both were smiling.

The woman walked down the street. Click, click, click, click. A red umbrella poised over her head. The mud from pavements splattered on her Italian shoes and fancy tights. She was dimly aware of admiring glances as she walked. Normally she savoured such glances, but today they meant little. Today she just wanted to get back to her flat. She'd have a bath, a good long soak, hey all those suds, girl. That's what she'd do. She had heard that it's what people do when they've had a sordid experience, they want to clean themselves, like women who have been raped scrub themselves with oven-cleaning pads. She wouldn't go that far, but she wanted a bath. A hot tub.

She'd soak it all away.

No, she'd need more than that to scrub it all away. She had an image of herself as a bundle of clothes on a scrubbing-board. That's what she needed.

Then she could soak. Only then. Maybe she'd change the water before she soaked so all the filth went down the plughole. Then she'd soak in clean water.

A bundle of clothes.

Then she'd sleep. She'd bathe, eat a light snack, and then sleep.

She was tired, she was hungry, she was cold. She walked across Albert Bridge. She glanced at the Clyde, icy, grey and flat, but with a million tiny ripples on the surface as the rain fell. She looked at the old Govan Ferry berthed against the piles and remembered it from her girlhood, plying backwards and forwards, cable drawn across a hundred yards of river, a lifeline between the north and south sides of the water.

She was frightened.

As well as everything else she was frightened. They said: 'Burn it.' They said: 'Take it some place and burn it.'

So she had taken it some place, the parcel, the brown paper, and inside his bloodsoaked clothing. She hadn't burned it because she couldn't. She tried, but the paper was wet, sodden in the drizzle. Nothing worked. In the end she left it there on the piece of waste ground in Hutchesontown. If waste ground was good enough for the body, a piece of waste ground was good enough for the clothing.

She should have just chucked it in the Clyde or

the Kelvin while it was still dark enough to do that and get away with it.

She had left the taxi, pretended to go into a close, then walked on to the waste ground and tried to light the bundle, but each match just fizzled out against the paper. Then she ignited the entire book of matches, and held the torch on the underside of the bundle. It scorched the paper a little, but that was all.

So she left them there just as dawn was breaking and began to walk back towards the town, searching the streets for a taxi. She walked past the dark red sandstone tenements, past the street corner bars with no windows and steel doors which stood like blockhouses on otherwise cleared land. Once there would have been tenements above and beside them, now they stood alone, with names like 'Paddy's Bar', 'Eddie's Bar', and signs on the outside saying 'Happy hour 7 P.M. to 8 P.M. All drinks at half price.'

Happy hour.

She continued to walk along Rutherglen Road, realizing that it was because she was being punished for failing that there were no taxis on the streets of Glasgow.

Click, click, click.

And she was being punished for being caught up in what she was caught up in. She never meant to be. Honest.

Click, click, click.

On her right-hand side were the deserted flats, smashed and vandalized, two-tone grey concrete. Built to a design approved by the Housing Committee because it had worked well in Marseilles with no sign of damp, but in just six months in the West of Scotland mushrooms were sprouting in people's living-room walls. Pretty soon after that they were abandoned and the ratepayers picked up the tab. Well, they had elected the idiots who composed the Housing Committee.

What's crime? she thought as she crossed the road towards the flats, turning her back on the Victorian monoliths of the Southern Necropolis. There's crimes on both sides of the law. She walked under the imposing edifice of the Greek Thompson church, with just the shell preserved as a listed building, which stood at the junction of Cathcart and Caledonia. She turned right. Pretty soon she'd see the white masts of the Carrick, she was close enough now to the centre of the town that she didn't need a taxi. Her flat was in the centre of town.

Click, click, click.

She wished she had had more matches. But who'd be interested in a bunch of clothes anyway. Nobody, 'course they wouldn't. Not anybody.

She felt weak with hunger. She hadn't eaten since yesterday evening. She hadn't slept properly, she wasn't sleeping these days. Always tired but never sleeping. Not properly, waking up feeling the need for a good night's rest.

She felt weak because she'd never seen a man killed before. Not in any way. Not like that. They didn't die like they die on television, sort of neatly folding up and looking like they're asleep. In life the head comes off, almost cleanly, but hangs there sort of hinged forwards, and the blood shooting up out of the neck and the body standing there, still standing, virtually headless.

She remembered somebody hitting her because she was screaming.

Then the body fell as if in slow motion. It all seemed to happen in slow motion.

Chapter Three

April 1st, 15.00 hours.

'Poster's fine,' said Findlater. 'You can distribute them as quickly as you like, Fabian.'

'Thank you, sir.' Donoghue took the rolled-up poster from Findlater's huge hands.

'Who are you putting on it?'

'The poster distribution? I thought . . .'

'The investigation, Fabian.'

'Oh, sorry. Well, Ray Sussock set the ball rolling, he's drawn the graveyard shift with Montgomerie, Abernethy's made a day shift contribution, King's on the back shift, he'll probably be in the building by now and there's work still to do.'

'It sounds as though you are using everybody?'

Donoghue nodded. 'I think I'll have to, sir. Everything else can wait.'

Findlater smiled. 'Better keep remarks like that confined within these walls, but I know what you mean. So there's nothing pressing?'

'No, sir, until this morning, which is conveniently a Monday, we seemed to be in the middle of a quiet period, a lull, and most of the team have grabbed the opportunity to blitz their paperwork. We have a series of raids on off-licences, a spate of burglaries, car thefts, a wilful fire-raising incident that's some weeks old now, I'm afraid the trail's getting cold on that one, we lost momentum. I don't want that to happen in this case.'

'Of course not. Absolutely not.' Findlater was a man of impressive bulk even for a policeman. He spoke slowly in a rich Highland brogue, which was almost musical to a lowlander's and Englishmen's ears. He had a gentle manner, not unusual in large men and certainly a common characteristic among Highlanders. The reputation for violence and aggression among the Scots is based wholly on the behaviour of small men from Glasgow and Edinburgh. Highlanders, as Findlater often reminded Donoghue by example, are gentle people. Another reason why Findlater exuded gentleness, Donoghue often thought, was because he had rarely, if ever, known violence. Nobody but a suicidal maniac would go up against a man who was six and a half feet tall and as stout as a boulder of Aberdeen granite. Findlater was a career cop, he'd never done anything else. Joining the force in his native Elgin as a cadet, he had reached the rank of Chief Superintendent of Glasgow's P Division in a respectable thirty years, not a black mark on his file, not a commendation to his credit. He was a solid cop. A cops' cop.

'In a sense this murder has been good for us,' said Donoghue, glancing round at Findlater's office, the same grey steel Scottish Office issue furniture, occasionally livened up with a blue door, or in two-tone grey. Scottish Office regulation floor covering of carpet squares which have to be watered with a watering can each morning to stop them peeling up at the corners as the central heating dries them. Findlater's office, though, was softened by plants, especially a large rubber plant, which Donoghue always associated with the flats of drug-taking students which he had had occasion to raid, and because of this the plant always seemed to him to be comically out of place in the top cop's office. Especially since the day that he put his head round Findlater's office door and caught the Chief Superintendent unawares having a most warm-hearted and amicable chat with the vegetable. The office was also softened by photographs of the Highlands, and a calendar with Highland scenery hung behind Findlater. The picture for April showed Ben Nevis still snow-capped, and, looking at the calendar over the shoulder of the Chief Superintendent, Donoghue noticed with interest that beside it was a fairly recent photograph of Findlater in a felt cap and waders, fly-fishing on the Tay.

Findlater had been appointed to P Division five years earlier and had immediately begun to make his office his home. It was the act of a man who was happy to have reached his last office and he noticeably relished the prospect. He was no longer young, and he had never been a 'thruster' anyway. His office was, as he had intended, homely, and his desktop an assuringly human shifting sand of papers and files.

'How do you mean – good for you?' he said.

'I mean it's going to galvanize us into action.'

Donoghue lit his pipe with his gold-plated cigarette lighter. 'The team has been getting its edges dulled.'

Findlater grunted. 'That's small compensation for the victim, but I know what you mean. We have no idea who he was?'

'As I said, no, and that's our first step. Abernethy spent the morning doing some good work eliminating the possibility that we knew the man either from Criminal Records or Missing Persons. Abernethy is convinced he's a foreigner for no tangible reason, but intangible reasons and impressions have borne fruit before now. Elka Willems is phoning round all the dentists in the city to see if they had a dental hygienist on Friday last, the twenty-ninth of March, and if so did they attend a man who fits the description of the deceased.'

'The cleanliness aspect is a puzzle, very odd, very odd indeed.'

'Very.' Donoghue pulled on his pipe. 'You know, I don't think it was done to hinder us, no attempt at washing away clues is what I mean. If they were going . . .'

'They?'

'Well, I assume there was at least one accomplice.'

'So long as it's not an all-excluding assumption.'

'It isn't at all, sir. I don't think that if they, or he or she, was going to go to that length of washing the body to throw us off the scent, then they would not have then left the body in such an open space, especially with the head positioned as it was. Somebody, or some organization, had the facilities and time to clean the corpse, dress it in new or clean clothes, and if they had time to do that they also had the means to dispose of it in such a way that it would never be found. No, it's a ritualistic killing and the body was intended to be found.'

'Certainly sounds like it.'

'It was also premeditated.'

'How so? Not an assault that went over the top?'

'The only item of clothing which wasn't new was the suit, though that was very clean . . . .'

'Yes, I recall that.' Findlater patted the file.

'I would suggest that that indicated somebody purchased the clothes prior to killing him. The suit was a bit of a problem, but they got round that as neatly as they could by using a clean one. It's almost as though they knew when he'd be collecting his suit from the drycleaner's.'

'Well, it's a puzzle and a half. You'll be keeping me informed, Fabian?'

'I will, sir.' Donoghue stood, collected the file from Findlater's desk, leaving a smoke screen in the air behind him as he strode the length of the CID corridor towards his own office.

The woman woke up and glanced at the alarm clock which stood on the cabinet beside her bed. Five-twenty P.M. Seven hours sleep, yet as always lately she woke up feeling so tired, so very, very tired.

She had entered her flat that morning, dragging one weary leg after the other, and had let herself thankfully into her hallway, shut the door behind her and sunk back against it. She had stripped and stepped into a bath as she had promised herself.

Then, with her arms feeling like lumps of wood, she had scrubbed herself as vigorously as she could, then soaked in the water, but had not changed the water as she thought she might. When she rinsed the tub she noticed, as she had on previous occasions, scores of hair in the water, she being in the habit of dunking her head and shampooing her hair while in the bath, rather than washing her hair separately, and these hairs were from her own scalp. She felt the same hollowness in her stomach when she saw just how many hairs she had lost, and then as before there was a frantic search of her head using two mirrors, but she couldn't locate a bald patch. Yet the hairs were just dropping out of her head.

She could not be going bald. She had long, lemon-coloured hair and life could not be that cruel. It just couldn't. She couldn't be handicapped at all, not in any way, not her, she could not possibly become one of those women who have to wear a wig because they are as bald as an egg, she wouldn't marry a violent drunk, she wouldn't give birth to a physically handicapped child or have a Down's Syndrome child, she wouldn't be in an accident and lose her legs, she wouldn't go down with multiple sclerosis and wheel herself about in an aluminium pram, she wouldn't have a stroke or get cancer and die young. She enjoyed being a girl, she had an attractive face, nice high cheekbones, blue eyes, she had a slim figure which was all in proportion. Men fancied her, she knew that, and she enjoyed being wanted. Life just wouldn't give her health and beauty just to snatch it away again. Not at the age of twenty-three.

Then she had turned back to the bath, the grey, soapy water, and pulled the plug chain. The water gurgled away in a whirlpool and the floating hairs gathered in the plug-hole. She picked up the loathsome mass and flushed it away down the toilet. She then patted herself dry and poured herself into bed, pulled the duvet over her, clutched the teddy-bear to her side and slept. When she awoke she felt just as tired as she felt when she had entered her flat earlier that day.

She glanced at the alarm clock; it stood obliquely to her vantage-point and she reached out and turned it towards her. As she withdrew her hand from the clock, she caught one of her fingernails on the edge of the cabinet, just slightly, just gently.

The nail lifted up off her finger.

It hinged up at the root. She found it quite painless and it didn't ride up a great deal. Just a quarter of an inch at the fingertip. But it rode up none the less and underneath the quick was a soft yellowing mass of pus.

The hollowness came again, excavating her chest and stomach. Her eyes began to water. She tried her other fingers. They too had loose nails, but none so loose as the one which lifted up like a trapdoor.

She knew there was something terribly wrong with her. It was as if her whole body, which had so far served her so well, had enabled her to compete successfully against other women, was just falling apart.

* * *

'I see. Well, thank you anyway. Good day.' Elka Willems replaced the telephone receiver on the rest and picked up her pen. On her pad she had written the names of the city's dentists, having culled the information from the yellow pages. Against Baker and Baker she wrote 'No dental hygienist surgery on Friday.' She wore her blonde hair in a bun, she was six feet tall and she still managed to look fetchingly attractive in the unflattering serge uniform of a WPC. Next on the list was Bitt and Snoddy, Dentists. She picked up the phone, dialled the number and said, 'Good afternoon, P Division Police at Charing Cross here. We're making inquiries in connection with a serious incident. Could you tell me if you had a dental hygienist's surgery on Friday or perhaps Thursday of last week? . . . You didn't. I see, thank you. Good day.' She wrote 'No surgery' at the side of Bitt and Snoddy. She sipped her coffee and picked up the phone again. It took her an hour to work through the list of dental surgeries which were listed in the Glasgow Yellow Pages. At the end of that hour she had made a separate list of twelve dentists who had held dental hygienist's surgeries on Friday, 29th March. These she had asked if they had treated a patient who was male, early middle-aged, and was perhaps wealthy, maybe even a private patient. The twelve receptionists took details of Elka Willem's request and agreed to consult the senior partner, they thought that in the circumstances the senior partner would allow them to call back with the names and addresses of any patient who might fit the description given.

Seven did call back at intervals during the afternoon.

Eventually Elka Willems had nine names and addresses which she kept on a separate sheet of paper. At the end of the period, half an hour after she had phoned the last dentist, and with her ear still burning from having the telephone pressed against it for the best part of an hour, she assumed that the nine names were all she was going to get. She re-wrote them in a more legible hand and took them upstairs to the CID corridor. She walked up to DI Donoghue's door and tapped on it. She waited, not daring to tap again, and eventually Donoghue said, 'Come in.' She opened the door and walked into the room.

Richard King sat in a chair in front of Donoghue's desk. He smiled at her as she entered. Donoghue on the other hand looked at the elegant WPC and raised his eyebrows.

'I've phoned the dentists as you asked me to, sir,' she said. 'Nine men were treated on Friday last who answer the description. I've listed them here, sir.' She handed the slip of paper to Donoghue. 'I've noted the name and address of the patients and also the surgery at which they were treated.'

'How many did you say?' Donoghue took the piece of paper.

'Nine, sir.'

'Nine.' Donoghue studied the names. 'I don't recognize any of the names, thought I might. Do you, Richard?'

King took the list, half standing in order to take

the paper from Donoghue's hand, who himself leant far forward across his desk.

'Will that be all, sir?' asked Elka Willems.

'Yes, thank you.' Donoghue allowed himself a brief smile at the tall, slender WPC. 'That will be all.'

Elka Willems left the room smoothly and silently.

'Dare say you can start checking those names,' said Donoghue. 'If all nine turn out to be alive and kicking then we're back to square one. One, just one, on the other hand may be missing from his place of residence.'

'And may well give us the break we are looking for.' King was twenty-four, chubby and bearded. Donoghue considered him to be one of the stronger members of the team, and just a short step from promotion to detective-sergeant. 'I'll get right on to it,' he said, copying the names in his own notepad. 'Spread far and wide,' he commented while writing. 'South side, east side, north side, Milngavie, West End . . .'

'How do you plan to attack them? Not alphabetically, I trust?'

'Oh no,' said King. 'Alphabetically would have me darting this way and that. Looking at the list, I think I'll go out to Milngavie, there's an address there, then I'll work my way to the south side, calling at the West End and north side addresses on the way.'

'Well, it's up to you. I never have and I never, I hope, will try to tell colleagues how to do the jobs I allocate to them. I pursue a policy of allocating work and then telling the individual to get on with it.

Having said that, how about following up a possibility rather than immediately starting a systematic checking of the names?'

'What do you mean, sir?' King handed the original list back to Donoghue and slipped his ballpoint into the circular wire spine of his notebook. 'Going to the West End addresses first?'

Donoghue nodded. 'Well, he was found in the West End. Not perhaps what I would call *the* West End, but I have noticed that estate agents are pushing the concept of the West End outwards to include the Maryhill Corridor.'

'It's worth checking first. I think you're right, sir. There are two addresses on this list which are in fact quite close to the place where the corpse was discovered.'

'It's up to you, of course, as I said. But it's a possibly productive short cut that I would be inclined to take.'

It was a short cut which King took, and which paid a handsome dividend.

Wilton Street cuts a high, long canyon of four-storey tenements, classy tenements with a narrow strip of garden between the ground floor flat and the pavement. Good enough, but even improved by the fact that most of the gardens are elevated so that a pedestrian cannot walk down Wilton Street and view the goings-on in the front rooms of the ground-floor properties as he passes. Less than a mile away in Partick, the tenements are smaller, they abut the pavement, pedestrians walk past the ground-floor windows. But that is Partick, this is Wilton Street, Kelvinbridge, built for the folk who live on the hill.

The flats in Wilton Street are large and spacious, five, six, seven rooms off a tiled 'wally' close. In its heyday the street was a middle-class enclave which of late has been taken over by absentee landlords who rent out flats to the unemployed, the students, or the homeless. The middle class have not given up without a fight. They still live in the street and the cul-de-sacs running off, and do so in large numbers: young professional men and women who prefer the inner city 'buzz' to suburban atrophy; elderly people, mainly women living alone in huge flats after their family has gone, staying on in what was once the home of their family.

The woman in the second-floor flat, right, opened her door just a matter of seconds after King had pressed her doorbell. He showed her his I/D and she showed him her shock and surprise and then her amusement. 'I can assure you, Mr King,' she said, 'I know of the exact whereabouts of my husband; he telephoned me not two minutes before you pressed the doorbell, to tell me he was working late at his office. That's why I was able to answer the doorbell so rapidly. I was still in the hallway having just spoken to my husband on the phone, which you see on the table behind me.'

King looked over her shoulder. He saw a long, wide hallway, a 'replica' telephone in brass imitation ivory standing on a highly polished wooden table with Queen Anne legs. The hallway had a heavy smell of wood polish and scented air freshener. It was heavily carpeted and King saw two white storage heaters standing against the wall. A child's tricycle lay on its side at the bottom end of the expanse of mother earth brown carpet. The woman was in her early thirties, she wore an Anti Nuclear Power T-shirt and denim jeans. Very folk on the hill.

'I'm sorry I alarmed you,' said King. 'It's just a routine inquiry.'

'No bother at all, Mr King. I'm not alarmed.' King liked her, she had a warm personality. She spoke, he noticed, with an accent which was higher-pitched than a Glasgow accent and with just the hint of a rising inflection. She was a Taysider.

'Well, again I'm sorry to have bothered you. Good day.' She shut the door gently as he turned back down the stair. Yes. He liked her.

The next address was literally around the corner from the first call. Both men probably did not know each other, but both had registered with the same dentist and both had had appointments with the same dental hygienist on the same day. The man who had called his wife to tell her he was going to be late home had an appointment at 10.30 A.M., and a man called Lurinski had kept an appointment at 3.30 P.M. that same day to have his teeth de-scaled and polished.

Lurinski lived in Dryborough Gardens, a cul-de-sac which drove off at right angles from Wilton Street. King located Lurinski's flat. It was two up left on a dark but cleanly kept close. The door was heavy and solid and black. 'Lurinski' was embossed on a highly polished metal plate screwed to the door just above the letter-box. He pressed the brass knob at the side of the door. Nothing happened, then he realized he had to pull it. This he did. Twice. He heard a bell jingle inside the flat. He'd never come across a bell-pull in daily use in a private house before. It must, he thought, be utterly original. As old as the building itself. The bell rang loudly but did not seem to provoke a response from within the property. He pulled the knob again.

Silence.

He began to turn away from the door, making a mental note to re-visit the address later that day, in the evening, when he heard a noise from behind the door. It was a slight, gentle noise of metal upon metal, a metal shovel being placed inside a metal pail and a brush placed in the pail beside the shovel. He heard the inner door open and then he heard a heavy bolt being drawn and one half of the storm doors, which divided the doorway in two, was opened. An elderly, bent, framed woman peered round the door at King.

'Aye?' she said. She held a carpet-beater in her hand.

'Police,' said King and flashed his I/D, holding it up for the woman's leisurely inspection.

'Aye?' she said, eventually.

'Is Mr Lurinski in?'

'No.'

'Do you know where he is?'

'No.'

'Do you know what time he'll be back?'

'No.'

'When did you see him last?'
'Monday.'
'Today's Monday, madam.'
'Aye.'
'You saw him last Monday, then?'
'Aye.'
'You don't stay here yourself then, no?'
'No.'
'You clean for him?'
'Aye,' said the woman. She was pinched-faced and had immediately reminded King of Ray Sussock's wife whom he had met once, briefly and a few years ago, and even this cleaning lady, giving little of herself as she was, King found to be infinitely more pleasant of nature than he recalled the ferocious Mrs Sussock as being.
'Just once a week. On Monday. But not at the Fair or Easter Monday or if Christmas or Hogmanay fall on a Monday.'
'I see,' said King, surprised at the sudden volunteering of information. 'You have a key, then?'
'Aye.'
'Do you normally see him when you come to your work?'
'Na.' Not even 'no', but 'na'. It was obviously back to the monosyllabic answers.
'So I take it that you see Mr Lurinski when he returns home at the end of his working day?'
'Aye.'
'When is that?'
'Maybe about five-thirty.'
'So he'll be back today at five-thirty?'

'I really couldn't say.'

'Why?'

'Well, he's not taken his car. His car keys are still hanging on the hook, and his office clothes are still in the wardrobe. So I don't know how he was dressed when he left for his work this morning.'

'Is that unusual?'

'Aye,' said the pinched-faced cleaner.

'Did – I mean, have you perhaps noticed anything else unusual this morning?'

'Well, his hat's still on the peg. He always wears a hat unless it's high summer, but this time of the year he'll want a hat.'

'Didn't that make you curious? All those things still here?'

'Aye, his top coat too, but I had so much to do I didn't have time to think, cleaning up, he had left the place in such a mess. So unusual.'

'Oh?'

'Aye,' said the woman. 'A lot of blood, blood in the drawing-room, trodden everywhere. It's taken me all day to clean it up.'

The flash bulb in the camera flashed and Donoghue blinked as yet another aspect of the locus of the offence was recorded for the police files. He shook his head to clear his vision and then focused on Elliot Bothwell, who was methodically dusting for latents, spreading iron filings, then delicately dusting them away from the surface with a squirrel hair brush, and not, so far as Donoghue could tell, discovering a great deal of helpful information. He had been so engaged for an hour by then and had highlighted nothing to be photographed.

The camera flashed again. On this occasion Donoghue had seen the scene of crime officer setting up the shot and had shut his eyes just before the picture was taken. 'I think that's me finished, sir. In here, I mean.'

'Very good,' said Donoghue. 'The rest of the house as well as this room if you'll be so good, please. Just record each room. I'm sorry that there isn't anything obvious to photograph.'

'Yes, sir.' The scene of crime officer left the room and cast a professional eye along the hallway looking for the best vantage-point.

Donoghue turned and called after him, 'Did you get the blood?'

The scene of crime officer, a slim man in his fifties, returned to the threshold of the room and glanced at the ceiling. There was a red circular stain about eighteen inches across and a number of small splashes around it. 'Yes, sir,' said the scene officer. 'Thoroughly recorded.'

'I would have cleaned up the blood from the ceiling,' the pinched-faced woman had said apologetically as she showed King the room, 'but I can't get a ladder to do it without moving the dining table, it's just in the way, but I can't move it alone, so I was waiting for Mr Lurinski to come home to lend a hand. Otherwise the whole house would be like a new pin. I'm good at my job.'

'I really don't think it will matter,' King had said as he led her gently towards the kitchen and out of the room which was clearly the locus of the offence and which now smelled dispiritingly of disinfectant and wood polish. He had asked the cleaner to wait in the kitchen and gone into the hall and picked up the telephone. He had held the phone with a handkerchief wrapped round the handle lest he disturb any latents, but he knew it was a futile gesture, since the woman's boast that she was good at her job seemed strongly founded in fact.

Donoghue left the dining-room shortly after the scene of crime officer and went into the kitchen where King still sat in the company of the cleaning lady. Donoghue looked about the kitchen with personal rather than professional interest. Latterly he had begun to develop an interest in Glaswegian architecture, particularly in domestic architecture, and in doing so had begun to find his modern, comfortable, centrally heated bungalow in Edinburgh dull, quite dull in fact. He noted the Lurinskis' household to be almost original: an enamel sink in front of the kitchen window, which looked out over the back court, two large taps, a wooden draining-board; a clothes-pulley hanging from the ceiling, sliding cupboards in the wall, a deep 'walk-in' cupboard lined with shelves; and, still, a cubby where in the early days of the house a maid, probably from Ireland or the Highlands, might keep her possessions and her change of clothing, and, unbelievably to late-twentieth-century values, would curl up and sleep each night, shutting herself away by sliding the panel shut. The ceiling enjoyed ornate plaster decoration around the edge of the room and also around the light cord, as in fact was the case in every room of the house.

'I'll just run through this once again, Mrs Dewey,' said King to the cleaning lady. 'Then I'll ask you to read it over and sign it.'

Donoghue watched the small Mrs Dewey nod twice as if she had slowly understood what King had said. Then she said, 'Will I get away on time, only I've a bus to catch and my sister's coming for her tea and who'll be paying me for my day's work?'

Donoghue left King at it. He was doing a good job, a diplomatic job, gently coaxing cooperation from the woman, who was evidently difficult, albeit unintentionally, and would be more so if she was told she would most probably not be thanked by anyone, let alone paid for her day's labour. Donoghue knew that women like Mrs Dewey, and fifteen-year-old girls who phone up the police full of hurt and indignation and say 'This is Sonia,' are the most difficult members of the public to deal with. King was doing a good job; he didn't need assistance.

Donoghue went into the drawing-room. It was original, like the rest of the house. Brown shutters on the windows, a solid, heavy fireplace. Old, heavy furniture. The house had survived the destructive period of the 1950s and 1960s, when people tore out the old fireplaces and replaced them with dinky gas heaters and plastered over the ornate ceilings and cornices. Looking over the house proved to be an amusing diversion, but he was a professional and there was work to be done. He went to see if Elliot Bothwell had turned up any latents yet.

* * *

'Only I thought I'd better call the polis,' said the man. His shirt was unbuttoned and hanging open and he was not at all self-conscious about his huge pink belly hanging over his trouser belt.

'Very right,' said Wanless. He stood looking at the bundle on the coffee table in the front room of the man's house. The house was spartan but comfortable, an uncashed, recently received Welfare Benefit cheque on the mantelpiece hinted at the man's source of income. 'The children found it?'

'Aye,' said the man. 'My weans and their friends, just out there on the waste ground, you can see from the window.' Paul Wanless glanced out of the window. A rectangular piece of waste ground, quarter of a mile long, two hundred yards deep, stood between the front of the man's close on Welsley Street and Rutherglen Road. Beyond Rutherglen Road was the lush green of Richmond Park, the trees bowing in the rain. 'Out there, aye?' said Wanless.

'Aye, just about dead centre. I mind when houses stood there. Rotten with damp, they were. A good thing it was when they came down.'

'When did you see the children playing with it?'

'About half an hour ago,' said the man, 'say about four o'clock. I called down to them out of the window and asked them what it was and they called back it was some clothes all covered with blood, so I went down to take a look, nearly broke my ankle crossing the rubble, but see those weans they hop about on it like mountain goats, so I saw what they meant, gathered it up and called the police. I thought you'd be interested in a pile of bloodsoaked clothing.'

'Thank you,' said Wanless, amused and amazed that the man had brought the bundle into his house and set it down on the coffee table, in the lounge, just next to the gas fire, which made the sickly sweet smell of blood rise and fill the room. But Wanless was twenty-eight, he'd been a cop for less than four years and people's behaviour still surprised him. 'Do you think you could show us exactly where your children found it?'

'Aye, no problem, son.'

Wanless gathered the parcel up, folding the paper down over the clothing.

'You see it's been scorched,' said the man, pointing to the side of the parcel. 'It's like someone tried to set it alight.'

'Seems like it,' said Wanless. He turned and carried the parcel down the stair, four storeys of narrow, winding stair. Clean though, very clean. Windows intact, no graffiti on the walls.

Piper waited in the area car. He got out as Wanless and the man appeared in the close mouth.

'In the boot with this,' said Wanless, 'rather than in the car.'

Piper opened the boot and Wanless placed the parcel beside the accident cones. Then he turned and followed the man across the rubble of the waste ground, picking his way gently and finally reaching a point which was, as the man had said, as close to dead centre as seemed possible without accurate measurement.

'Just about here,' the man said, standing in the rain, scorning the cold, still with his shirt open. 'Next to that big stone, see, there's a book of matches, I didn't notice them before.' Wanless stooped to pick up the book of matches. He opened it, many of the matches were still there, but all had been ignited and the phosphorous had welded the matches together as though all had been flared off at once. He searched the ground and picked up six individual matches which seemed to have come from the same book.

'Looks like somebody put one or two matches to the bundle and didn't get anywhere, so they burnt the whole lot to try and get the clothes burning,' said the man.

'Looks like it.' Wanless folded the matches shut. On the cover it said Zambesi Club, Hope Street. The logo was a palm tree.

Chapter Four

Monday, 17.00 hours.

Donoghue read the reports, some of which had been typed, others awaited typing, but were submitted to him none the less for his urgent edification in legible longhand. These he would read, absorb, and then place in the basket marked 'For typing'.

He felt the inquiry was beginning to take shape. Tests showed that the blood on the ceiling of the Lurinski household was of the same blood group as the blood group of the deceased, as given in Dr Reynolds's report. The blood on the clothing found in a bundle on a demolition site in Hutchesontown was also of the same blood group. A wallet was found in the inside pocket of the bloodstained clothing. The wallet contained in excess of a hundred pounds, a photograph of the owner and his address in Dryborough Gardens, G20.

Donoghue began to doodle on his notepad and then he wrote 'He knew them.' He felt that Lurinski had to know his attackers because there was no sign of forced entry at his house, and no sign of a struggle within the house. He had let them in, or they had a key, and Lurinski was then quite at ease with them, because when his back was turned and when he was quite relaxed someone had swung a cleaver or similar, and had succeeded in severing Lurinski's head almost completely from his body, sufficiently to let a jet of blood geyser out and splatter the ceiling. Then the corpse had been stripped, washed and dressed in new clothing and a recently dry cleaned suit. The corpse had been carried a few hundred yards to some waste ground where it was laid out, a sheet drawn over it and the head placed on top of the sheet. It lay there until it was found by Hamilton at 06.00, eleven hours ago.

'I'm sure I would have seen it, sir,' Hamilton had said. 'Even from the pavement. I'm certain it wasn't there when I passed at 00.30 hours or thereabouts.'

Then Donoghue had asked him if anybody was on the streets at that time in the morning?

'Milk boys, sir, young boys, teenagers, who help out on milk rounds, a few all-night buses, early buses, minicabs, regular taxis, various stand-by teams of the city's departments, Housing, Welfare, Direct Works, then there's emergency gas and electricity fitters. The city doesn't really sleep at night, sir, not in the sense of total shutdown, it just assumes a different character. Also there are people who just can't sleep and get dressed and go for a walk.'

'Yes, yes,' Donoghue had murmured as he recalled the unusual amount of activity which goes on at night from the time he pounded the beat as a fresh-faced young cop. That conversation with Hamilton was snatched at the beginning of the day, just before Hamilton signed off and went home. Now at the end of his working day, just prior to handing over the inquiry to the back shift, he wrote on his pad 'Somebody may have seen something. A house to house?'

He reached for his pipe and filled it with his special mix tobacco from his leather pouch. The fill would accompany him for most of his hour-long journey home to Edinburgh, that and Radio Four on the Rover's stereo.

There was a tap on his door. He put his pipe down and said, 'Come in.'

Richard King entered. 'Plenty of dabs in the house, sir,' he said after the preliminaries. 'Problem is that they all belong to Mrs Dewey, the conscientious cleaner. She left as many dabs as she swept away. Elliot Bothwell did manage to find two that she missed. He lifted them and sent them to the collator who'll run them through our computer.' He glanced at the clock which stood on the wall behind Donoghue's desk. 'Doubt if we'll get a result today, computer services shut down at five o'clock. Must be nice to work nine to five, Monday to Friday at that.'

'It's all we need,' said Donoghue. 'We've always got plenty to be getting on with and, if not, we have the legislation to hold a suspect until we can get a comeback from the computers. Even if we nick him on Friday night. Our own Criminal Records is a twenty-four-hour facility, maybe they've got some matching prints on the good old-fashioned card index system.'

'Well, they've already been sent off, sir, we'll find out in the morning if the latents Elliot found are on record. If they're not known to computer services they won't be in the drums downstairs.'

'Fair enough. Have you had a chance to glance through these reports?' Donoghue patted the folder.

'Not fully, sir.'

'If you'd acquaint yourself with the known facts at your earliest convenience. I've been having a last read through. I think he knew his attackers.'

'Most murder victims do, sir.'

'Yes. What I mean specifically is that he knew them, but did not believe that they threatened him. No sign of forced entry, no sign of struggle.'

'I see, sir.'

'The treatment of the corpse after death is bizarre, washing it. Why do that? Dress it in new clothing. Why?'

King shook his head and added, 'Why even bother to carry it outside the house at all? It's not as if they were going anywhere, just a couple of hundred yards down the street. It would have been easier and less risky just to leave it and let it be found by the bustling Mrs Dewey.'

'She still wouldn't have called us until she'd given him a good dust and polishing. But you're quite right, it's another question to be answered. The whole thing is ritualistic.'

'Isn't it.'

'I'm sure somebody saw something. You cannot carry a body for two hundred yards without attracting attention. Not in Wilton Street, not even in the dead hours. There's always something going off down there, if it's only the druggies setting up their three A.M. deals. They're not likely to come forward anyway, but still, even so, I cannot believe that nobody saw anything.'

King nodded. 'I'd be inclined to agree, sir. Lurinski was not a small man. It would have needed at least two strong men to carry him, a third to carry the head and the sheet. What do we know about Lurinski, sir?'

'He was an accountant. He held a position with Biddulph and Co. Mr Biddulph, of Biddulph and Co., will be at home to you after 6.30 P.M.'

'To me, sir?'

'Yes, King.' Donhoghue smiled. 'To you, sir. I wish you to interview Mr Biddulph about his deceased colleague Mr Lurinski. You know what we are looking for as well as me. Anything you can dig up, really. At this stage of the game we don't know what's relevant and what isn't. I phoned Mr Biddulph at his place of work earlier this afternoon, just caught him as he was about to leave, there was a business card in Lurinski's wallet . . .'

'You found the wallet, sir?'

'Oh yes, you won't know, his wallet and all the clothing he was wearing was found on yet another bit of waste ground south of the water late this afternoon. Details in the folder.'

'Very good, sir.'

'Biddulph sounded distressed and shocked. He has an address in Lenzie.'

'Right, sir.'

'Address in the file. There's an establishment called the Zambesi Club to be visited. The person who attempted to incinerate Lurinski's clothing used a book of matches from the Zambesi Club. There may be a connection, there may not. Perhaps Montgomerie, who's coming on later, night shift with Ray Sussock, I believe, perhaps he could visit the club. I have the distinct impression that clubland is his er . . .'

'Scene,' King prompted.

'Yes. Exactly.'

'Do we know Lurinski?'

'Good question and the answer is no. We do not know him and he is not known nationally. The police national computer came back with a "no trace". Managed to get that out of the computer services before they went home for their tea and six o'clock news at least.'

'What about the Saltcoats Hotel connection? Anybody picked that up?'

'Abernethy's on it at the moment,' Donoghue replied.

'The clothing I mentioned earlier is still at Forensic. Dr Kay's agreed to work late and she may well come back at any time with a bit of gold dust for us, but so far she hasn't called.'

'I'll bear that in mind, sir.'

'The mysterious figure running along the towpath intrigues me,' said Donoghue. 'I'd like to know a little bit more about him or her.'

'That was the only movement around at the time,

according to Hamilton's report,' King commented. 'I'd also be surprised if the figure is not connected.'

'Well, we'll see what we shall see.' Donoghue stood and handed the folder to King. 'Abernethy will let you know of the outcome of his visit. If you could call on Mr Biddulph, pass on to Montgomerie my request that he acquaint himself with the Zambesi, heaven knows he may already be a regular patron, and I for once, Mr King, am going home more or less on time.' He lit his pipe with his gold-plated lighter. 'If anything breaks you can call me at home at any time, otherwise I'll leave the CID department in general and the Lurinski inquiry in particular in your capable hands.'

King tucked the file under his arm. 'Very good, sir.'

Abernethy felt the man was sneering at him. The attitude that in the armed services is called 'silent contempt'.

'Two months ago,' said the man in tweed who even from Abernethy's side of the desk smelled richly of after-shave. The man had a way of looking down his nose while sitting bolt upright and managed to make Abernethy feel the gangly overgrown teenager he was often taken for.

The man smiled. He had a red face, he was plump and he wore an expensive-looking sports jacket. His office was decorated in a manner which gave it a sense of depth and solidity, dark browns, burgundy reds, maroons. His desk was annoyingly neat. 'January was a good month for us,' he said. 'As I recall.

We are not a family hotel, you see, Mr Abernethy, despite the coastal location. Most of our clients are businessmen. But I'm confident the receptionist will . . .'

The phone on his desk rang. The man remained sitting upright, smiling at Abernethy, letting the phone ring for an over-long time. Abernethy suspected that the hotelier must be a real tyrant to have to work for. Then he thought: No. No, he wouldn't be a tyrant, because a tyrant would have snatched the phone after it had hardly started to ring and would bark down it; despite everything there was something honest and up front about petty dictators even though they might wear their weakness and shortcomings like armour plate. This man, Abernethy felt, would be more inclined to be downright spiteful, wilfully undermining the self-confidence of his employees, especially the vulnerable younger ones who'd end up believing they could do nothing right and leave his employment with a 'not up to the job' type of reference with which to start seeking alternative work. And the job situation being what it was in the West of Scotland, he continued to get away with it. Eventually he extended a lazy arm, picked up the phone and said, 'Mr Kilroy here,' moving his tongue round the words like he might move it around a hardboiled sweet. 'I see,' he said, scribbling on his pad, 'I see, yes . . . thank you, Mary. That will be all.' He put the phone down. Then to Abernethy: 'The receptionist has traced the reservation, as I was confident that she'd be able to. Mr Lurinski came here for a weekend, the last weekend in January of this year. He took a double room. He and his lady companion arrived on Friday evening, had dinner at the hotel and departed on Sunday after breakfast.'

Abernethy scribbled on his notepad. 'Did anything unusual or untowards occur during his stay, anything that involved him?'

'Not that I noticed, nor that I was aware of.'

'Did his companion give a name?'

'They booked in as Mr and Mrs Lurinski, according to the receptionist. I remember them in fact, they seemed a little nervous and unrelaxed in each other's company, a little too eager to please the other. They were not married, otherwise they would have been more natural together. I supppose one could say it was an honest to God tried and tested, dirty weekend.'

'Can you describe his companion? His partner?'

'Younger than he was. In her twenties, I'd say. He was middle-aged I seem to recall. Is that correct? Was Mr Lurinski middle-aged?'

'Yes,' said Abernethy, 'he was. You didn't note her name?'

'As I already told you,' said Kilroy with a trace of impatience.

'Yes, I wondered if you could recall a Christian name, you didn't overhear him address her, no?'

'No.'

Abernethy couldn't see the way forward. He heard the clock tick. A car outside.

'I could tell you which room they were in.'

Abernethy glared at him. Now Kilroy was laughing at him.

'I hardly think it matters,' said Abernethy coldly. 'I dare say it's been occupied since.'

'Oh yes. I do good business. Full most of the year.'

'Yes, the business community, I remember.'

'I don't remember anything about their stay, Mr Abernethy, or about anything else being reported. Some guests stick in your mind, either because of their behaviour during their stay or because of what the chambermaids find in their room after the guests' departure. I assume that this means that Mr Lurinski and partner behaved quietly and kept themselves to themselves and left the room clean and tidy.'

Abernethy scribbled, and that he did so amused Kilroy, who could not think anything he had told the nervous police officer could possibly be of use. So he added quietly, 'She was oriental.'

Abernethy looked up.

'If you had asked me if there was something, anything at all, I remember about Mr Lurinski and partner, I would have told you of the lady's racial extraction earlier. But you didn't ask.'

'Oriental,' echoed Abernethy coldly.

'Oriental. In a sense they made an odd couple. He was tallish, heavily built, thin-faced, middle-aged, conservative in dress, and she was petite, slim, youngish, in her mid-twenties, also smartly dressed, a pinstriped suit, very fetching on a young lady, but I had the distinct impression that she had a more flamboyant side to her wardrobe. Another thing that made them stand out was their attitude to each other.'

'Yes, very nervous. You said that, Mr Kilroy.'

'There's a little more to it, in fact. You see, we get many middle-aged businessmen bringing young women to the hotel. The men work hard at impressing the women, flash money about; the girls show themselves off, but otherwise they suffer the weekend with resignation, the girls, that is. Such couples talk a lot but don't look at each other much, not a lot of eye contact. They are also self-conscious. Believe me, I have been in this business a long time, "guest-watching" is my hobby. I can tell everything about my guests just by looking at them. I know whether they're on top, when they're having a bad time, I know if they're loners or just alone, when the wives get dragged here while the husbands are attending a convention, I can tell if the marriage is breaking up or solid, and I can do that before they've been here thirty minutes. Not bad.'

'Not bad.' But Abernethy wondered how the man could ever find out if he was right or wrong if his guests stayed only for two or three nights at a time.

'Now Lurinski and his partner, they spoke little, but so far as I can recall spent a lot of time looking at each other, they were not self-conscious in that they were concerned about what effect they were having on each other. They had each other and the world could turn without them.'

'They cared about each other deeply?' said Abernethy.

'They were in love,' replied Kilroy, his voice

bearing the authoritative stamp of an experienced guest-watcher. 'At least they were well on their way to reaching that elusive state.'

Richard King drove out to Lenzie. The Biddulph residence was a split-level house, all angles, with huge sheets of glass instead of front walls. There was an alpine garden in front of the house falling all the way to the cherry trees next to the wall which separated the property from the public thoroughfare. A long gravel drive ran up the side of the garden to a double garage which stood next to the house. Two cars stood in the drive, both BMWs, both less than twelve months old. One was a small sports saloon in light blue, the other car was maroon in colour and was the largest model of the BMW range. The cars said everything except 'his and hers'. King parked the police heap at the bottom of the drive and walked up the gravel.

'Well, yes, we did have an argument,' said Biddulph, 'and I find it somewhat annoying to have to tell you the truth, Mr King.'

'Annoying, sir?'

'Please don't misunderstand me. I am personally sympathetic, I make no bones about it, but I feel that I'd rather an old-established and respectable firm of accountants like ourselves continue to enjoy the address of Royal Exchange Square with all the links the name has with our city's economic history and with all that the name implies, rather than have an address in Nelson Mandela Place.'

King raised his eyebrows.

'You're not sympathetic, Mr King?' Biddulph walked away from the sideboard holding a large gin and tonic. Behind him a pane of glass ran the whole length of the wall, beyond which was a high vaulted room containing an indoor swimming pool. At the side of the pool a woman lay on a sun-bed. King felt as if he was in a goldfish bowl; the house was divided by glass interior walls, the whole front of the house was one huge pane of glass which King noticed, when he got closer to the house, was angled forward at the bottom so that the room couldn't be looked into from the street. King looked again at the woman on the sun-bed and presumed her to be Mrs Biddulph; she was as old as her husband and was losing the fight against years and King felt that she should really have resigned gracefully long ago.

'Sure you won't have a drink?'

'I'm sure, sir, thank you,' King said. 'I don't know whether I'm aware of the issue sufficiently to be able to say where my sympathies lie.'

'Well, that's diplomatic if nothing else.' Biddulph sat heavily on the leather chesterfield, his stomach rose up and pushed out his silk shirt above his belt. His drink was a large one, generous with the gin, light on the tonic. He had a ruddy complexion and was perspiring about the brow.

You're hitting it too hard, thought King. Next you'll be telling me it helps you unwind.

'It helps me unwind,' said Biddulph, noticing King looking at his glass. 'I've done my day's work. Did well today, wound up a company and had all the ninety-day redundancy notices sent out. Nice bit of business, really. No, of course you don't understand the issues, how on earth could you? All right, the city has made a powerful point in renaming the square Nelson Mandela Place because that's where the South African Consulate is, but why penalize us? Businessmen are conservative, especially if they deal in money. Financiers, accountants, banking houses, investment brokers, we are all frightened of anything which smacks of change by force, and established customers are reluctant to send us business because of our new address.'

'I can't see why that should be.' King sat back. 'I mean, the issue is clear-cut.'

'Of course it is,' said Biddulph. 'The Republic of South Africa is wrong, the ANC is right. End of story. But the point is that businessmen who would happily spend a day with their families in Nelson Mandela Park, which used to be called Roukenglen or Strathclyde Park, are the self-same men who are reluctant to send business to people who have an address in Nelson Mandela Place. Names are important and have associations. If you are making golfing wear, for instance, it will sell better if you call it the Gleneagles Golfing Jacket, for example, than it will sell if you call it the Motherwell Golfing Jacket, even though the product and price are identical. Why? Because Gleneagles means golf, health, success, money and media coverage. Motherwell means steel and dust and pollution and high unemployment. So you call your product the Gleneagles jacket. It's the way people's minds work.

There's often no logic involved, and it is often a question of prejudice, either positive or negative prejudice. In the case of our clients the prejudice is not racial or political, it's a prejudice towards established usage; it's a liking of old street names to be continued and prejudice against the street name being changed because of a fashionable political trend, no matter how ethically correct that trend may be. Royal Exchange Square has been Royal Exchange Square for a hundred and fifty years, the name has always been appropriate and relevant, and would have continued to be so. How relevant Nelson Mandela Place is going to be a hundred and fifty years from now I don't know. Not very, I think. You get some idea of what my feelings are if you could imagine such famous streets as Threadneedle Street and Fleet Street in London, or Times Square in New York, being renamed after the leader of the ANC, and done so in a fit of political high-mindedness.'

'I confess I still think it was a brave gesture,' said King.

'I think it was brave as well, but I think a more appropriate location could have been chosen, like a park as I said earlier.' Biddulph gulped down his gin and tonic. 'Let me also say that if when Nelson Mandela comes to Glasgow to accept the freedom of the city which was conferred upon him some years ago, I shall be one of the doubtless thousands of people who will be cheering in George Square when he stands on the steps of the City Chambers with his gown and scroll. I just wish they hadn't changed the name of the street where my business is located, that's all. Today was good, but it was work from an established client, days like today are getting rare. Some of my neighbours have moved out and have set up again in Blythswood Square. The brave gesture of the elected representatives is costing me money. And that's what I was arguing about with Samuel Lurinski. Dead, you say?'

King nodded. 'I'm afraid so.' He watched Mrs Biddulph drag herself up off the sun-bed and waddle, King could think of no other word, for even with his personal striving for magnanimity being influenced by his Quaker wife, Rosemary, Mrs Biddulph's rear view was to him wholly gooselike, and with her ridiculously short legs, even as a young woman, she would have suffered badly from 'duck's disease'.

'Murdered?' said Biddulph.

'This morning,' said King. 'At least, that's when the body was discovered.'

'I wondered why he didn't turn up for work or phone in sick, and then your Inspector Donnachie . . .'

'Donaghue.'

'Yes, Donoghue, then he phoned. Still in shock.' He took a stiff slug from his drink. Ice rattled in the glass. 'You wanted to know about the argument I was having with Sam. Argument was too strong a word, really; well, I sounded his opinion about whether we should cut and run.'

'Cut and run?'

'Sell the premises for what we can get for them,

do like the others have done, you know, open up again in premises with an address which has a solid and permanent feel to it. I was surprised by his reaction.'

'Oh?'

'It was not dissimilar to what I assume your own opinion of the issue is, Mr King. Basically, Sam's attitude was that moving away would be to endorse racism. He said it would be easier if we just moved from Royal Exchange Square to Nelson Mandela Place instead of moving from Royal Exchange Square to Blythswood Square. That surprised me. I was also surprised by the depth of feeling he revealed, the passion held about the issue. I've known Sam for nearly twenty years. I've never known him harbour feelings as intense as those feelings he showed on Friday afternoon. He didn't show feelings of any kind when the name change was announced, didn't make any contribution to the discussion about the issue, just got on with his job. Then on Friday I said, "What do you think about moving from these premises and seeing if business picks up?" Well, Mr King, he exploded with rage. Sam isn't a partner in the firm, he is an employee. If a junior had spoken like that he'd have got his jotters, no questions. I think I was too surprised at Sam's evident feelings to be offended at his manner. It was almost as though he had a personal stake in the matter, something I was and still am quite unaware of. Sure you won't . . .' Biddulph held his glass up.

'No, thank you again,' said King. He glanced out

of the front window. Inside the house you could look out, outside you couldn't see in; the landscaped gardens fell down to the road in a series of terraces, and at the bottom of the garden was the row of cherry trees just coming into flower. In full bloom they would form a blazing pink ribbon screening the house from the road. It was a different world entirely from King's own small house, still half decorated, still with wood stacked in the kitchen which he had bought the previous winter intent on making shelves for Rosemary, who always dressed in pastel shades and refused to wear jeans, who never complained, who was always waiting for him when he came home, no matter how late. He thought the Biddulphs really lived in two separate worlds; he with his gin, she with her solarium.

'Murdered?' said Biddulph. He heaved himself up from the chair and crossed the carpet to the drinks cabinet. 'Sam . . .' he shook his head. 'How . . .'

'I can't tell you yet, sir,' said King.

'Fair enough.' The Beefeater bottle was turned bottom upwards as Biddulph poured another stiff one. Again the tonic was little more than a token additive. 'Just a couple before dinner. Then I'll finish off at the golf club.'

'You'll be driving there?'

'Yes. I'll be safe enough. Especially after a meal to soak it up. Drink doesn't affect me, I've been a drinker all my days, need it to keep going. Mrs Biddulph says I'm a better driver when I've had a drink.'

It was the logic of an alcoholic, King thought, and

was reminded of a car accident he had once attended. It turned out that two St Andrews' yuppies had got legless and decided that the safe way to get home was to drive each other's cars, and they ended up racing on the highway. One was killed and the other never again drove anything more powerful than a wheelchair.

'Mr Lurinski,' said King, 'he'd been with you for some time?'

'Twenty years or so, being the time I have known him. Entered the firm as a junior, came from an Insurance Broker's. He was a committed financier, passionately interested in money as a commodity, not interested in making it, if you see the difference. He had a strong sense of right and wrong, a moralistic young man. Came of his family, I suppose. Only child of parents who were members of the Free Church. Calvinistic, fire-and-brimstone stuff. Grandfather was a European, hence his name, eastern European, and sometimes I thought Sam had a distinct Slavonic look about him. Sam didn't inherit his parents' religious conviction, but he did inherit their sense of frugality. Visited his home once, the home he had grown up in, amazing place, like stepping back into a different time, not the slightest bit of modernization. Be a lovely place to do up.' Biddulph looked over the top of his glass at King. 'Hey, now there's a thought, be coming on the market soon, won't it, he's got no dependents. If I got in quick with a cash offer, well, fine apartment, just waiting to be modernized, I could buy it for a song, tear out all that wood, rip out the fireplace and that antiquated sink unit, put in new fancy panelling and central heating. I could turn a tidy profit on that house if I get my oar in smartly.'

'Mr Lurinski . . .' King forced the conversation back on to the rails.

'Sam, yes.' Biddulph gulped his gin. 'Staid sort of chap, not a sparkling sense of humour, didn't drink, never touched a drop. Not a drop.' By now Biddulph was saying 'dwop' and King knew the interview was drawing towards the end of its usefulness. King thought he had until Biddulph finished the glass. Any further interviewing would have to be done at Biddulph's place of work when, King presumed, the man would be sober. 'Yes, strongly moralistic, and there are some sharks in this business, they wouldn't wait to stab you in the back, they wouldn't put themselves out so much, oh no, the dreaded vorpal blade can come at you from the front and you watch them smile as they spill your blood. Sam was aware of the gullible and the vulnerable. I remember him, at his interview, sober-faced, black suit and tie, and in the interview he revealed the one and only trace of cynicism I was ever to hear from him.'

'Oh?'

'Yes. He said of his job with the Insurance Brokerage, "We sell a lot of rubbish to a lot of fools with a lot of money." That's why he wanted out. It was immoral. I gave him a start and he just got on with it. He was meticulous, careful, punctual, tended to go the second mile, a good man, made a name for himself, could have moved on to other firms for more money, but he stayed with us. We could have given him a partnership, but he did not seem to want it. Not ambitious at all. Murdered?'

'Yes.'

'Who?'

Biddulph swayed towards the door, but King said that he could see himself out, thank you.

She let herself into the flat as though she owned the place. She hadn't moved in, she had a flat of her own, but there was something unnerving, something pushy about the way she had been carrying herself about his flat of late. 'You in?'

Montgomerie levered himself on to his right elbow and said, 'Yes.'

'Still in bed?' she called. 'Do you know it's the back of seven? Some of us have done a day's work.'

'And some of us work shifts,' said Montgomerie to himself as he sank back on to the pillow.

She burst into the bedroom and flung the curtains wide. The sudden flood of light hurt his eyes.

'Get up!' she said and left the room.

'Bloody hell,' murmured Montgomerie. Truly amazed. He'd met her two weeks previously. 'Teach gym,' she said, smiling over her iced Coke. 'If you can't do, you teach; if you can't teach, you teach gym.'

He had said, 'That right?'

Then she had said, after a pause, 'Well, Y.P.O.M.?'

'Mine, if you like,' he said, and that was just three hours after meeting her for the first time, not quite his personal best, but good enough for a chance meeting on a rainy day.

Now, on the evening of 1st April, still not fully awake, listening to Miss banging and dropping his kitchen utensils and walking heavily on her heels along his hall, he had to concede that enjoying success with women is not without pitfalls.

The pounding from the room above woke Sussock. Momentarily he was disoriented; oh yes, this was his flat, his bedsit, it must be evening, yes, that morning he'd come home, then he'd driven to her house in Langside, she was out, he'd forgotten she was day shift all week so he'd had to spend the day in his miserable room after all.

They forgot about people's social life when they invented the shift system.

He turned over and put his head under the pillow, but he couldn't escape the music. He glanced at his watch. Seven P.M. He'd slept for six hours. Good enough, at least he'd got some good nourishing sleep before the office workers came home and turned on their music centres.

Boom, boom, boom, boom.

It might not be so bad if he could hear the music, but it was just the base notes that came through the ceiling.

Boom, boom.

He glanced about him. The bedsit was as bright and spacious as he could make it, but in fairness he hadn't much to work with. A single bed, an armchair, a table, a black and white television standing on an old orange crate. A wardrobe, a high ceiling. The ceiling . . .

Boom, boom, boom.

He rolled out of bed. The chill air pinched his skin. He pulled on a pair of trousers and, leaving himself stripped to the waist, went down the hall to the bathroom, clutching his sponge-bag and towel. The landlord was a Polish displaced person who had fixed the water heater so that it only gave out hot water in the morning and only then between the hours of seven and eight, which was not a great deal of use to a cop who worked shifts. But he washed anyway and brushed his teeth. He went back to his room and pulled on a shirt and a jersey.

Boom, boom, boom.

He went to the kitchen. He had a few cans and some bread and a tea-bag. The kitchen was dark and vast, a single window set behind massive bars looked out across a lawn to a high stone wall. Somebody had cleared out his cans and bitten into his cheese. Again.

He leaned against the table and sagged his head. It was not the value of the products he resented, it was that he had to live in such conditions; it was that at the age of fifty-five, after a lifetime's police service, he hadn't got a home to go to.

He left the vast house and went to Harry's. He liked Harry. He could have gone to half a dozen similar shops, but he went to Harry's. Harry was tall and good-looking and warm of personality, he wore a purple turban and kept racks of Indian videos as well as racks and racks of food in his mini-market.

He always treated people as though they were human beings, and he had time for everyone.

'Hi, Ray,' said Harry as Sussock entered the shop.

'Hi.' Sussock lifted a wire basket from the stack next to the till.

'How's it going,' Harry said, punching the till.

'One day at a time,' said Sussock, 'same as always.'

Back at the bedsit he cooked up and then drove to Rutherglen. He pulled up outside a bungalow and walked down the drive. He knocked on the door.

The door was opened. A slim, dark-haired boy of twenty stood in the doorway. He was dressed in black, black T-shirt, black velvet trousers, black gym shoes. He wore bracelets on his wrists, he had two rings in each ear. He smelled of perfume. He stood on the step and smiled at Sussock. A second boy, same age, a little taller, angelic of face, but blonde instead of dark, came silently up behind the first and nudged the first with his groin as he slipped his hand round his waist. He also smiled at Sussock. Then the first boy stopped smiling. His expression hardened. He said, 'I really don't think Mummy will be happy that you've called on us, Daddy.'

'Tough.' Sussock felt his right fist clench. He relaxed it. It wasn't his fault that his son had turned out like this. He'd gone to London like many young men and had, like most young men, returned, but unlike most young men he had come back walking a strange walk and with an all-knowing smile. Soon after he had returned Sussock discovered him sitting in the front room of the house painting his finger-nails, having taken the hair from the back of his hands with his mother's lotion. He'd looked up and smiled and called Sussock 'Daddy' for the first time ever.

'Mummy,' the young man called without taking his eyes off Sussock. 'It's Daddy.'

From somewhere within the house a woman wailed a high note of protest. Then she ran to the door, Sussock heard her coming, banging doors, stamping feet, the young men stood aside as she approached and when she appeared she was as he had always remembered, barely five feet tall, with a pinched, screwed-up face.

'What are you doing here?' She spat the words. 'You were never any good to me and Sammy, was he, Sammy? Always out catching robbers, no time for us, isn't that right, Sammy?'

'Yes, Mummy,' said the dark-haired young man.

'Never saw you, day in, day out, you were never here, never where you should be.'

Sussock started up the steps.

'Oh, coming in, are you?'

Sussock stepped over the threshold.

'Still think you own the place?'

The woman backed off as he entered the house.

'You don't either,' said Sussock.

'Not be long, not be long,' chanted the woman, backing towards the living-room.

Sussock walked past her and went into a small room just off the hall. He took a plastic bag from his pocket and began to fill it with a few items of his, mostly clothing, and a light raincoat for the coming summer.

'Take it all, take all of it,' shouted the shrew from

behind the front room door. 'Give it to charity, help the poor.' She kicked the door.

Sussock left the house.

'Try not to call again soon,' said his son as he slammed the door behind Sussock.

He flung the plastic bag on the back seat of his car and drove to Langside. He pulled up at the kerb and went up the stair. He stopped at a door with 'Willems' on and he pressed the bell.

The door was opened almost immediately. She had changed out of her uniform and now wore jeans and a yellow top. Her blonde hair had been released from its bun and now hung about her shoulders.

'I didn't expect you,' she said, smiling, standing aside to let him in. 'So it's a nice surprise for me.'

They kissed briefly as they passed. She shut the door behind him and followed him into the room.

'You look done in,' she said. 'Just finished? Oh no, you're on the night shift, aren't you?'

'Yes. I'm just about to start. I've just been to Rutherglen to collect a few things. Still the same as ever. What a mess I'm in. I feel I've been cheated of something.'

'Grab a pew, old Sussock. I'll fix you a coffee.' Sussock sank into the armchair.

'And stop moping. No room for self-pitying wimps in my life, just for men who can square up to their problems.'

Sussock smiled. 'Coffee sounds great.'

She left the room and he heard her switching the kettle on and putting the mugs down on the working surface.

He glanced round the room. It was the 'room' of a room and kitchen, once the home for a whole family, often sharing the same bed, and was not unlike his childhood home in the old Gorbals, the screams in the night, the blood on the stair in the morning. Now her home was the home of one person, the room was the living-room and bedroom, the bed being tucked into a recess, books on shelves, the coffee table in the centre of the room, the carpet, the Van Gogh print on the wall. There was an entrance hall, and then the long, narrow kitchen, a toilet off, and a shower room. It did one person very well.

She brought two mugs of steaming coffee into the room and handed one to him. She curled up at his feet and hooked her right arm over his left knee. He stroked her head.

'You eaten?' she said.

'Yes.'

'I could fix you something if you want. It's no trouble.'

'I'm all right really,' he said. 'Thanks anyway.'

'I draw night shift next week,' she said, sipping her coffee. 'I don't mind it so much, especially if it's quiet. I walk the streets shining my torch about, drop in for coffee at the bus depot or the fire station, or the council garage. It's handy having a city centre beat, there's always somewhere you can go to get out of the rain or take the weight off your feet for half an hour, have a warm-up and a blether.'

'The graveyard shift,' said Sussock. 'You can keep it.'

She ran her hand down his shin.

Chapter Five

Monday 19.00 hours–Tuesday 02.30 hours.

Abernethy had driven back from Saltcoats via the coast road. It was the long way round through Inverkip and Gourock. He liked driving by the sea, he liked the shore. He was unhappy deep inland away from the crash of the surf and he guessed he'd be equally unhappy far out at sea, but he loved the shore, where the water constantly moved against the land. He had once read an article which had been written in layman's language about an anthropological theory which told that man, of all the primates, stood tall and had thick legs because primitive man was a shallow water dweller, using the shallows as a place to retreat when threatened by the land-based predators, though never venturing far enough away from the shallows to be threatened by marine predators. The buoyancy of the water enabled him to stand upright. Abernethy had no idea whether the theory was sound or not, but it had filled two pages of a magazine and had kept him amused on a train journey from Edinburgh to Glasgow. One day he would have a small house with a garden which ran down to the coastline.

It was dark as he drove. He could easily make out

the lights of Dunoon across the water, the flashing lights of the buoys in the channel, and he saw the sweep of the light beam of Cloch lighthouse as he drove towards it. Round the Tail of the Bank he saw the lights of a Caledonian MacBrayne steamer as she plied towards Greenock. In the bay at Ashton he saw that the braver owners had already put their yachts on their moorings.

He drove through Greenock, passed the shipyards with their ever-present smell of rust which penetrated his car. Out in the Clyde he saw a newly completed oil rig anchored and awaiting tow down river, and presumably round the north coast of Scotland to oil fields in the North Sea. He drove along the south bank of the river, past the Bishopton turn-off, past the entry to the suspension bridge, past the airport, past the first exit to Paisley.

A jet passenger plane flew low overhead on its approach to the runway.

Clyde Tunnel or the Kingston Bridge? He took the tunnel. As he plunged into it he noticed the smog of carbon monoxide hover near the roof. He switched off the ventilation system to avoid drawing fumes into the car and accelerated, clearing the tunnel as rapidly as he could. The traffic was light; he would only go into the tunnel when traffic was light.

He drove along Dumbarton Road, a canyon of four-storey tenements, of pubs, small shops, which, after Partick Cross, became Argyle Street and out to reveal the Art Gallery and Museum, and above, on the hill floodlit at night, the University of Glasgow.

Then he drove into Sauchiehall Street, more tenements, hotels varying in standard from top line to cheap lodgings used by the city to house homeless families, and a crescent of early Victorian houses occupied as business premises by solicitors, accountants, architects. There were restaurants and good pubs. Abernethy turned left just before the motorway and then immediately left again into the rear entrance of P Division Police Station. There were no parking spaces. He put the car in Chief Superintendent Findlater's space. It was the end of the working day, the Chief Superintendent would be away long ago.

He went into the building, signed in, and checked his pigeonhole for messages. He went to the 'canteen', really just a room with four tables and a kitchen off. Two traffic cops sat at one of the tables drinking coffee, their white caps on the table in front of them. Abernethy nodded to them. They nodded back. The canteen was a pleasant place when things were not too crowded. When it was a crush, most officers just accepted the need to get in and get out. Fast.

Abernethy hustled himself a coffee and took it upstairs to the CID corridor. He took off his coat and sat at his desk and began to write up his account of his interview with the hotelier in Saltcoats. His conclusion was that the deceased had spent a weekend there, about two months previously. He had taken a double room which he had shared with a girl of oriental extraction. Theirs had apparently been a relationship of quality. He left the report in Donoghue's pigeonhole, reasoning that the Inspector would wish to apprise himself of the contents sooner, rather than wait for it to come back from the typing pool later in the day.

Abernethy went home by bus. He stayed south of the water in a three apartment. He let himself in quietly and then tapped on one of the doors inside the flat.

'That you?' said a voice from inside the gloom.

'Yes.'

'What time is it?'

'Not that late. Coming up nine o'clock,' said Abernethy.

'That you?'

'Yes.'

'What's it like out?'

'Little bit of rain.'

'What time is it?'

'Nine o'clock, thereabouts.'

'Fine out?'

'Touch of rain.'

'Been at your work, aye?'

'Aye. I've been at my work.'

'Fine out?'

'Rained a little, easing off now.'

'What's the time?'

'Nine o'clock.'

'Good night, son.'

'Good night, Dad,' said Abernethy.

'It could be a two-hander,' said Montgomerie.

'You reckon?'

King stood. Montgomerie sat. They both held cups of coffee. Occasionally Montgomerie turned and looked at his reflection in the window. He was tall, good mane of hair, downturned moustache; he liked women and, if they didn't like him, they certainly liked being seen with him.

As often as not this suited Montgomerie to perfection.

King had waited for Montgomerie to arrive to commence the graveyard shift at 22.00 hours. He had written up his account of the interview with Biddulph, and had seen Abernethy's report in Donoghue's pigeonhole and had taken it out and read it. When Montgomerie came on duty, King handed him the file and allowed him half an hour to digest the nuts and bolts of the inquiry.

'So you see,' said King, 'the only lead so far not followed is the Zambesi Club connection. You and Ray Sussock are on night shift, we thought that of the two of you perhaps you would be more suitable. Ray wouldn't, er, blend as well as you.'

'Getting paid to go to the dancing? Some job, this.' Montgomerie put his feet up on the desk and held his mug of coffee in his lap. He looked warmly at King. Then he said, 'Could be a two-hander.'

'You reckon?'

'Well, you never know what you are going into in a situation like this.'

'It's not a two-hander,' said King. He said it wasn't a two-hander because he wanted to finish on time and he knew what Montgomerie was going to suggest.

'Look at it, you're going in blind, never knowing who you're going to run into, one bloke going into a discotheque.' Montgomerie shook his head. 'Has to rouse suspicion. Men hunt in packs.'

'Oh yes? I didn't need a pack to find my wife, our eyes met across the "late returns" desk of the public library and she took a quid off me.'

'Take it from me, my son. Men go in packs, at least in pairs.'

'Pairs. I doubt if Ray . . .'

'I was thinking of the two of us.'

'Us! Hey, wait a minute, just a wee minute, big man . . .'

'No problem, I'll have you home on time, no sweat. Ray will be in soon, he can look after the shop. Grab your coat, you and I will gyrate.'

'Gyrate?' said King. 'I thought we were going to the dancing?'

The Zambesi Club stood on the corner of West Nile and Bath Street. In the nineteenth century the building was a bank, now the ground floor was a plush bar, still with the original mosaic tiled floor, and drink instead of money changed hands across the long, heavily polished wooden counter. Overhead fans turned slowly, but these, King immediately realized, were for effect. They were definitely not needed in Glasgow on the night of April 1st.

Montgomerie strode confidently into the bar, King shorter, chubbier, followed and he watched with amusement at the head-turning effect his tall, good-looking colleague had on the young women who sat in the wicker chairs behind the marble-topped tables, between the door and the gantry.

Music played. There were vacant stools at the gantry.

'Gin and tonic twice,' said Montgomerie, sliding on to a velvet-topped chromium-plated stool.

King clambered up on to the next stool. He looked around him. He rarely drank but was familiar with drinking dens with sawdust on the floor because he regularly pushed open the doors to such places in the line of duty. Being a cop, he invariably silenced them, felt the collar, huckled the individual out into the street with somebody invariably calling 'See you in sixty days, Jimmy,' bounced the pinch into the 'jeep' and away. But this bar, the Zambesi, was definitely unfamiliar territory.

A young man in a starched white shirt and black tie brought the drinks to Montgomerie. A measure of gin in tall glasses full of ice, a bottle of tonic with each glass put down on soft paper mats which said Zambesi and had the same palm tree motif in the centre. King poured the tonic into his gin and began to drink it. Then he choked when he saw how much Montgomerie paid for the round.

Montgomerie smiled and picked up the receipt, always given automatically in a place like the Zambesi. 'Our expenses are good,' he said.

'Dare say this is your idea of a good job,' said King.

'There are worse,' Montgomerie swilled the drink round in the tall slender glass. 'You could have been a cop, for example. That would slay me.'

King smiled and began to take delicate sips of a drink which had become too expensive to consume any other way.

Montgomerie pulled a packet of long thin cigars from his jacket pocket and offered one to King. King shook his head. Montgomerie took one and put it to his lips. He took the book of matches which had been found close to the bundle of Lurinski's clothing. A girl in a fetching blue dress came up to the gantry and stood beside Montgomerie gently rubbing her shoulder teasingly against his and equally gently rattling her empty glass on the gantry top. Montgomerie winked at King. Eventually the girl bought her own drink and went back to her seat. Montgomerie said, 'It happens all the time.' King was just pleased that he was married and wanted very badly to go home.

Montgomerie raised a finger slightly. Just sufficient to attract attention, not enough to seem imperious. 'Do you have a light?' he asked as the barman approached. The barman slipped his hand inside his hip pocket and pulled out a lighter. He flicked it into life and held the flame steady as Montgomerie pulled the cigar alight.

'Thanks,' said Montgomerie.

'Pleasure,' said the barman.

'Run out of these?' Montgomerie tossed the book of matches on to the counter.

The barman picked it up. 'Never seen these before. Well, how's this, Spike,' he addressed the other barman.

Spike came over.

'See these before, Spike?'

Spike nodded. He said they weren't for widespread distribution, might get them downstairs. Then Spike went to the other end of the gantry to refuse to serve a man in his fifties, who King had noticed earlier trying to chat up every spring chicken in sight. The man was unsteady on his feet and glazed across the eyes. Spike waved his hand in the air and two men, whom King had taken to be customers, left their seats and escorted the ageing raver smoothly across the mosaic and into the street. Few people noticed the incident and King was not unimpressed.

'Downstairs?' Montgomerie jabbed a finger downwards.

'The dancing,' said the barman. 'Black Hole of Calcutta, laughingly called a dance hall. Used to be the vaults of the bank so I believe, but you get a good idea of the size.'

King smiled.

Montgomerie said, 'Why should they give out complimentary books of matches down there and not up here? What's the difference?'

'They're not really given out down there either,' said the barman. 'It's just that the boss has an office down there, small cubbyhole of a place just behind the bar. Entertains guests, talks business, clinches deals, and it's to business associates that he gives out gimmicky gifts like ballpoint pens with the club name on. I've seen them, but not the book of matches, that's the first time I've seen matches.'

'I see,' said Montgomerie, pocketing the book of matches. 'What's your boss's name?'

The barman stopped looking friendly and started to look worried.

'Police,' said Montgomerie and flashed his I/D.

'Stein,' said the barman, leaning closer. 'But don't say I said so, OK. You got the information from the Business Registry, that's if anyone asks.'

'If anyone asks,' said Montgomerie.

'Who else might be given these matches, or who might have access to them? Anybody?'

'Just the staff, I guess,' said the barman. 'If they work below. But then I'm only the piano-player.'

'Not a regular?'

'Three nights a week, sir.'

'Student?'

The barman nodded. 'Law.'

'That's a good ticket to be on,' said Montgomerie. 'I have a law degree. The people I was at uni with are pulling down five times what I'm earning now.'

'Something going on here, sir?' asked the barman, still leaning close.

'Could be,' said King. 'Could also be that we're going up a blind alley. Anyway, take our advice and stay back from anything dodgy and stick to your studies.'

The young man smiled and nodded. Then he went away to serve an overweight girl with a close-cropped hair-style.

'Going below?' said King.

'Don't know. What do you think?'

'Can't see the point if it's going to be as crowded

as that, dancing in the vaults, ugh! Won't see anything, won't be able to hear anything.'

'Could make it official.'

'And say what?'

'That we found a box of Zambesi Club matches close to the location where a murdered man's clothing was found. It appeared that an attempt had been made to set fire to the clothing.'

'It'll rattle a few cages if nothing else.'

'Only if there's a connection,' said Montgomerie. 'But I'd be keen to give it a whirl.'

They left the bar, went outside and down a sunken alleyway. At the end of the alley two steel doors and two bouncers stood between King and Montgomerie and the Zambesi dance floor.

'Evening gents.' One of the bouncers eyed King and Montgomerie. His manner was cautious, verging on the reverential. Montgomerie nodded and slid sideways past the bouncers. King followed. Inside was a long corridor, dimly lit. Sound came from the far end of the corridor.

'Never knew we had "cop" written all over us,' said Montgomerie.

'It gets stamped on your forehead when you join the club,' said King, 'but only certain types can see it.'

Montgomerie walked up to the cash desk and paid the entrance fee for two. Not cheap.

'Do you think this place is making a courageous attempt to pay off the National Debt by itself?' said King, but Montgomerie was already on the dance floor. King walked after him.

A drunken girl flung herself at Montgomerie. He grabbed her by the waist and lifted her sideways towards King. She draped her arms around King's neck, slobbered a few kisses over him before tottering off the floor.

Montgomerie and King approached the small bar which stood adjacent to the dance floor. Montgomerie reduced the weight of his wallet against two drinks of modest measure and he and King leant against the bar. Behind the gantry was a mirror. Montgomerie looked at his own reflection. The mirror had bands of frosted glass one inch wide running vertically, dividing up the plain mirror surface every two inches.

'One-way,' he mouthed to King.

King nodded. Such mirrors are not by any means uncommon in Glasgow pubs and clubs, nor are they uncommon in the city's police stations. In fact they are becoming more and more common. Cops can see out, the public cannot see in. A member of the public will walk into a police station and stand at the uniform bar and see his or her own reflection, but not what lies behind the mirror. He will ring for attention, gaze at the missing persons posters, the wanted posters, the murder posters, the Colorado Beetle posters. Eventually, having established his own time and terms, a police officer in a crisp white shirt will walk around the side of the mirror and say, 'Yes?'

'So who's behind it?' King yelled over the noise.

Montgomerie looked about him, young people

dancing in couples, singles and groups. A disc jockey sitting on a raised platform.

Montgomerie shouted, 'Not doing a lot here.'

King nodded. He was anxious to go. The cellar of the Zambesi was not 'him'.

Montgomerie surveyed the gantry. No complimentary books of matches. He leaned forward and beckoned a bar girl towards him. She was dressed in yellow and black and had a Zambesi Club motif on her blouse.

'Mr Stein, please,' shouted Montgomerie.

The girl's face flashed in the strobe lights.

'Who wants him?' she yelled back.

Montgomerie showed her his I/D. The girl nodded, smiled and slipped away, moving towards the end of the bar. The mirror behind the bar wasn't wholly one-way and Montgomerie caught a glimpse of yellow as she moved behind the vertical frosted glass at the rear of the mirror. Then he watched the yellow move back again to the door and the girl came out from behind the mirror and approached Montgomerie. She smiled at Montgomerie, went to the very edge of the gantry and opened a hinged section. She beckoned the cops to follow her, and led them along the rows of beer pumps and upturned spirit bottles. Behind the gantry, behind the one-way mirror, was a cramped office. A man sat at a small desk. The girl said, 'Police, Mr Stein,' and left the office, shutting the door behind her. The effect of shutting the door was outstanding to the cops. They looked at each other.

'Soundproofing,' said the man by means of explanation.

Montgomerie didn't like the man. King tried to summon his wife's Quaker principle of looking for the good in every man, but he too found it difficult to like Mr Stein.

Stein, both cops thought, could be anywhere between forty-five and sixty-five. He had light smooth skin and a small amount of fair hair, but his age was concealed by obesity and thick-lensed spectacles. King would not permit himself to think unkind thoughts, having already that day dismissed a lady's walk as a waddle, but Montgomerie thought the man looked like a pear. His head and face were wide at the bottom and seemed to taper upwards. His body too was pear-like, vast about his middle, tapering up to his shoulders. What both cops disliked about the man was the evident smugness and self-satisfaction he enjoyed. He wasn't running a discotheque and bar because he was interested in music and trendy drinks, as a younger man might have done. He was running the business first and last because it was a means of making easy money. The Zambesi was fronted by students and young barmaids; behind the scene, sitting on the coffers, was Mr Stein, easily old enough to be parent to any one of his customers. He was exploiting the young. 'Yes, gentlemen,' he said and gold flashed inside his mouth.

'DC King and DC Montgomerie,' said Montgomerie. He held out his I/D for Stein's inspection.

Stein examined the I/D card and then sniffed imperiously.

'We hope you can help us in connection with a serious crime.'

'I'd be pleased to,' said Stein, smiling and putting his head slightly to one side.

King was unnerved by the man's forced pleasantness and felt that the man could easily turn savage and violent at the slightest provocation. He looked round the office. Small and cramped. He looked at the mirror, and had an uninterrupted view of the girls serving behind the bar, the dancers, as Montgomerie had said, gyrating. The flashing lights penetrated the office and Stein's face flashed in and out of darkness and the gold in his mouth flashed on and off. King thought the top of Stein's desk was too neat; even at this time of night, in the middle of his working period, everything on the desktop seemed to be in its place, three pencils sharply pointed lay parallel to the ruler, which lay parallel to the side of the desk. Such desktops made King cringe, and Montgomerie too preferred desktops which were a human mess of papers and files and coffee mugs.

Stein continued to smile in the dark and light, the light and dark.

King had to remind himself suddenly where he was. In a cellar in a Glasgow discotheque. Outside, just above his head, was West Nile Street, solid nineteenth-century buildings, the beginning of the city's grid system, orange buses, yellow and blue buses, London style taxicabs. Montgomerie wondered if he was quick enough to punch Stein and get away with it in the frequently brief instances of complete darkness.

'It's in connection with these matches, sir,' said Montgomerie. He took the book of matches and dropped them on the desk between the telephone and Stein's jotting pad. The lights flashed, black and white, light and dark, but the darkness didn't last long enough to conceal a look of alarm in Stein's eyes. Even behind the thick glasses the eyes revealed a look of shock.

'They're mine,' he said.

'We are aware of that, sir,' said King. 'We also understand that these books of matches are not given away freely or distributed in a way that they could be picked up by the public. We understand that they are given only to personal contacts of yours, sir.'

Stein shrugged. 'Well, yes, that's correct.'

'Do you know of a man by the name of Lurinski?' Montgomerie asked.

'No . . . no.' Stein stammered and looked shaken.

Both cops knew they had struck gold.

'You see, why we ask,' said King as Montgomerie reached forward and picked up the book of matches, 'is that earlier today, early this morning, at about three A.M., Mr Lurinski's body was found on a piece of waste ground in Maryhill. There were one or two odd things about him which made us think it was a suspicious death.'

'Such as the fact that his head had been detached from his body and was left sitting on his chest,' said Montgomerie.

'Doesn't happen if a guy dies of a heart attack,' said King.

'And the deceased was wearing new clothing.' Montgomerie wrapped the book of matches in his handkerchief and slipped them in his pocket.

'What has this to do with me?' Stein was panicking. A bead of sweat ran from his forehead over his cheek.

'We don't know,' said King.

'We give in,' said Montgomerie. 'What has it to do with you?'

Stein leapt to his feet. 'Get out! Get out!' He was about five and a half feet tall. Fat rippled beneath his shirt. 'I will not be intimidated.'

'We've still got the dabs to lift,' said Montgomerie, patting his pocket.

'Dabs?'

'Fingerprints,' said King. 'They often tell us quite a lot.'

'Well, you'll find mine on them because I just touched them.'

'Of course,' said Montgomerie. 'We'd expect to find your latents on them.'

'But who else's might we find?' King turned to go.

'We'd be particularly interested to lift the latents of the persons unknown who used these matches in an attempt to set fire to a bundle of clothing on a demolition site in Hutchesontown.' Montgomerie followed King.

'Clothing?' Stein addressed the backs of the cops. But only Montgomerie turned, chiselled features and a down-turned moustache. 'Lurinski's clothing, sir. Came into our possession, bloody but quite undamaged at about 16.00 hours. Perhaps we'll be seeing you later, sir.'

Richard King got home at half past midnight. His wife had waited up for him. She wore her hair in a bun, had a cotton shirt and printed cotton dress, she wore black shoes with a modest heel. She had waited up for him because she had considered it her wifely duty to do so, never mind that she had a home to run and a young child to tend. She thought that if her husband could not sleep, then she should not. She took his coat and hat and he kissed her because he loved her very much and he was so, so happy to be home, where she was, and was glad to be away from the lights and noise and the painted women of the Zambesi Club.

'Richard?' She looked hurt. 'Is that alcohol on your breath? And there's lipstick on your collar.'

Rosemary went to the kitchen and brought a mug of hot tea which she pressed into his hand.

King, tired, heavy-eyed, said he could explain. But she sat in the armchair and bowed her head, the way she did when she was disappointed.

Abernethy lay in bed listening to the rain patter and splatter on the glass. He had enjoyed the drive along the coast, much better than coming back across Fenwick Moor. Then he thought about Samuel Lurinski, a middle-aged man, and his oriental girl-friend much younger than he, both deeply in love, sharing a room in a hotel in Saltcoats, off season.

* * *

She staggered up the street. Her legs felt like cotton wool. People looked at her, some pitying, some disgusted. She wanted to say something, say that she was not drunk, not drunk like you think, that she could come back and explain, later she could explain, but now she had to get to the G.R.I., just up there, up Castle Street. Climbing up the hill, Duke Street and George Street lights behind her.

Her head swam.

Her vision blurred.

She staggered on. She suddenly remembered that she had not let the cat out, then she remembered she had left the door of her flat open. So the cat would go out. She laughed. How ridiculous, after all this, how ridiculous to worry that she had not put the cat out.

People moved away from her. She could see the spire of the Cathedral against the night sky. She remembered how the Cathedral is a lot bigger than it looks. From the road it looks like a big church, and only as you walk down the winding path to it do you realize how huge it is, how inside it is vast, with small chapels in the basement and a large crypt.

She staggered on.

Stein had promised her a doing if she fouled up. She wondered how he had found out so quickly that she hadn't been able to burn the clothes. How had he known? She was sure she wasn't followed. It was just the crack of dawn, nobody about. The matches he had given her didn't work, with the rain drizzling like it was. Even if somebody had found the clothing, how had they linked it to that poor guy whose head was taken off when he wasn't looking. And that was . . .

My God, it was only this morning.

But Stein had kept his promise. He'd sent Spike round and the other guy, who looked so harmless but who was a vicious little ned. She staggered. She smiled because she could see the G.R.I.

Not far to go. One foot in front of the other. Keep walking, got to keep walking, got to keep the teeth gritted.

Afterwards she'd go and see her mother. Her mother lived in a two-room-and-kitchen in Parkhead. She had grown up there. A two-room-and-kitchen to a three apartment in Tailor's Court. Not bad.

What was the name of the vicious ned?

One foot in front of the other.

Not far now. Keep going, hen. Don't bother about these folk, you can go back and tell them you're not drunk. Go back one day and tell them about Spike and the vicious little ned . . .

Castlemilk Fats.

That's what they called him. Lean as a rake, not a pick on him. From 'the milk', that's why they called him Castlemilk Fats.

So you can do that, hen, you can go back and tell them about Spike and Castlemilk Fats, who work the upstairs bar at the club, coming round, kicking the door in, no problem, doors in 'new build' property are like matchwood. One good kick and they're in, no matter how many locks are on them.

Castlemilk Fats said, 'Mr Stein sent us.'

Spike had said, 'He's not best pleased. He said we had to carry out his promise.'

She staggered towards the Casualty sign. She saw an ambulance crew walk towards her. She held her stomach. There was blood in her mouth.

Christ, you took a doing tonight, girl. You took a good doing.

Over in the south side of the city a restaurant stood empty. It was the Bay Leaf Chinese Restaurant. It was closed each Monday. Inside the restaurant a timer ticked. The timer was linked to an industrial detonator, which was strapped to a jerrican of petrol. The jerrican of petrol was only half full, had to be like that to provide plenty of vapour. The jerrican was surrounded by plastic containers of cooking oil.

About five hundred gallons of cooking oil.

The timer stopped ticking at 02.30 hours, Tuesday, April 2nd.

Chapter Six

Tuesday, April 2nd, 03.00–07.15 hours.

By the time that Ray Sussock reached the scene of the Code 9 the fire was well beyond control. It was a raging inferno which had completely engulfed the small restaurant. Occasionally flames bellowed out beyond the main body of the fire as they were fired by sudden explosions within the building. It was a major incident attended by six appliances of the Fire Brigade. Tentacles of hose lay across the road, some held by teams of firemen, others set on tripods, but so far as Sussock could tell the heat generated by the blaze was so intense that the water from the hoses evaporated before it was able to penetrate the flames. One fire hose was played on the wall of the adjacent building, other fire officers rescued the elderly or infirm as nearby houses were evacuated.

'It's all we can do to contain the blaze,' said the Chief Fire Officer to Sussock. Sussock thought the man remarkably calm.

'I don't think there's anything else we can do,' said Sussock. 'Perhaps you'd let us know when you have the blaze out, and especially if you can locate the cause.'

The Fire Chief nodded. 'The seat of the fire is in the basement,' he said. 'I can tell you that now just by looking at the flame pattern. It was obvious when we got here that the building was burning from the ground up.'

Sussock walked back to the car. As he climbed into the vehicle he saw uniformed constables moving among the crowd, asking for witnesses and occasionally writing in their notebooks. He drove back to P Division, signed in, went upstairs to the CID corridor, went to his office, took off his hat and coat and sat at his desk. He took a fresh file from the bottom drawer of his desk, coded it with the next number in the year's sequence and on top wrote 'Fire, Ayr Road, Clarkston', and then dated it. Inside, on the first continuation sheet, he wrote a paragraph recording the time of information received and a summary of his visit to the scene of the blaze. Then he closed the file. He re-read the report submitted by Abernethy, which he had taken from Donoghue's pigeonhole and which concluded that the deceased Lurinski had a lady-friend of oriental extraction. He had just finished reading the report as Montgomerie knocked on his door and walked into his office.

'Thought I heard you come in, Sarge.'

Sussock wondered how Montgomerie could be so cheery at this hour of the morning. But then Montgomerie was a young man; graveyard shifts are for young men.

'I've just made a breakthrough in the Lurinski case,' he announced.

'You have?'

'Well, myself and Dick King.' Montgomerie placed his report on Sussock's desk.

Sussock thought that Montgomerie looked pleased with himself. Perhaps Montgomerie had good reason to look pleased, no doubt the report would tell him whether he had or not. He picked up the report, but in doing so found himself wishing that it had been King who had written it. He knew from previous experience that whereas King's reports were full and 'fleshed out', contained a 'voice', not a judgement, had reasoned opinion, and had on occasion had the accolade bestowed upon them of being duplicated and distributed to the cadets as an example of good report writing. Montgomerie's reports were, by comparison, generally nuts and bolts only. Often they posed as many questions as they answered.

Montgomerie sat on the chair in front of Sussock's desk.

'Sit down,' said the older man drily as he began to read the report.

Montgomerie smiled uncomfortably. 'Sorry, Sarge, force of habit. Simple association, you know: chair, sit?'

'Aye,' growled Sussock, already half way through Montgomerie's report, which was not disappointing his expectations, being meat picked to the bone. Reading Montgomerie's report was like looking at the skeleton of an animal and having to depend on imagination to gain some semblance of idea as to what the beast looked like. He had read the report in less than a minute.

'Stein esq, of the Zambesi Club, showed guilt when told about the matches and seemed alarmed that they could be linked to the Lurinski killing,' quoted Sussock from Montgomerie's conclusion, which wasn't a great deal shorter than the report itself.

'Yes,' said Montgomerie.

'Alarmed?'

Montgomerie nodded. 'Dick King will bear me out. We put our heads together before I wrote the report. Stein was put out by our call. We thought we'd rattle his cage and I think we succeeded.'

'I see.' Sussock put the report down. 'As always, we have to follow up your reports with a question and answer session. I wish you'd remember that while you might know or suspect a great deal, your colleagues can only know and suspect what you share with them. Which is often not a great deal.'

Montgomerie smiled a what-can-I-say smile, and Sussock felt there to be little percentage in labouring the point. The issue had been taken up with Montgomerie in the past with little effect. He wondered where to go from here.

'I thought I'd dig around the files and see what, if anything, we've got on Stein,' said Montgomerie. 'If the shift stays reasonably quiet it would be a good use of time.'

Sussock nodded. 'Can't do any harm. We might have something in the Rotadex, which will keep us going until Computer Services opens for business at 09.00 hours.'

'Anything else on, Sarge?'

'Fire in the south side.' Sussock pinched his eyes together at the bridge of his nose. He glanced at his watch. Not yet 03.30 and he was fighting off sleep already. 'Fire Officer will let us know if there's anything in it for us.'

'What's the building involved?'

'Some Chinese restaurant.' Then he looked up. He thought of Lurinski's oriental lady-friend. No. There couldn't be a connection. Could there? No. of course not. 'Montgomerie.'

'Sarge.'

'See when you're checking the Rotadex, let's look for any connection between Lurinski or Stein with Chinese restaurants.'

'You think this is connected?'

Sussock patted Abernethy's report. 'Did you read this, Abernethy's report?'

'I did not.'

'Lurinski had an oriental lady-friend. He possibly still has if she doesn't know of his murder.'

'I see.'

'Well, it's a long shot. As you say, it's a quiet shift, there's time to play the long shots, which have come off before now.'

Montgomerie nodded. 'I'll get right on it.' He stood and left Sussock's office. When he had gone, politely shutting the door behind him, Sussock put his feet on the desk, folded his arms across his chest and shut his eyes. He wasn't going to sleep, he told himself, he was just going to stop himself trying to stay awake.

It was perhaps half an hour later, at the point where there was a little cramp in his legs, at the point where he was half asleep, just half asleep, at the point where noises, somebody walking along the corridor, an ambulance's klaxon passing in the street, seemed to be further away than usual, seemed to be from a different existence, it was at that point that the phone on his desk rang.

'She's semi-conscious,' said the voice, soft-spoken, male, self-confident, a Highland accent, an accent which put Sussock in mind of Chief Superintendent Findlater, who at that moment, thought Sussock, would be doing the civilized thing and slumbering peacefully.

'A young female, you say.' Sussock scribbled on his pad.

'Yes,' said the Highlander. 'That is to say a young adult female, probably in her early to mid twenties. She has sustained severe trauma to the head and the body, bruising and probably fractured ribs. In a word, somebody gave her a good kicking.'

'Casualty, G.R.I.?' Sussock scribbled.

'That's it.'

'And you are, sir?'

'Dr Monroe.'

'Oh, I think we've met before, sir,' said Sussock.

'Probably have. It's been my experience that you tend to meet up with the same members of other professions if you do night shift long enough; the world is smaller at night and other professions will put themselves out more than the same team would during the day. How's your shift going?'

'Quite quiet so far,' said Sussock. 'How's it been with you?'

'Quiet for the first few hours, then we got run off our feet. The city went mental when the dancing came out. It's quietened down again now. This young lady I'm phoning about, she came in when it was going like a fair and we had to attend to the "bleeders", as we say. The young lady was damaged, but she wasn't bleeding so she waited. I've just treated her.'

'You'll be admitting her?'

'Yes, just for observation in the first instance. If you wish to interview her, Records will tell you which ward she's on. I have sedated so there'll be no point in sending anybody round tonight. She'll be able to speak tomorrow, that is later today, if you see what I mean.'

'Do you think she'll make a statement?'

'Hard to say,' said Monroe. 'She was semi-conscious and a lot of resentment was coming out. She might feel different in the cold light of day. She's not married, at least there's no ring on her finger, so she might make a complaint. What I mean is that I tend to despair of the number of women I sew up and plaster back into some sort of shape, only to see them return to their husbands who seem bent on re-shaping them. The number of women in this city who think that any husband is better than no husband at all . . . well, it takes some getting used to.'

Sussock sighed. 'Aye,' he said. 'How long do you think she'll be in hospital, sir?'

'Hard to tell. As far as the injuries are concerned she may be discharged later today, after lunch, especially if there's no indication of head injury. The problem is that there's something else here, skin blemishes, and a scalp condition which seems to be making her hair fall out. Her fingernails are loose and there's pus under them. I'm going to ask the Registrar to have a look at her when he comes on duty later this morning. Depending on what he says, she could be detained a little longer.'

'I see.' Sussock scribbled. 'Did you get the lady's name, sir?'

'Yes, she is one Louisa Salisbury.'

'That's a nice name.'

'Isn't it? Very English-sounding, but she's as Glasgow as the Molindinar, going by her accent.'

'I see. Well, it seems she might have a story to tell. I'll ask a WPC to call and speak to her sometime during the day shift. Thank you for phoning us.'

Montgomerie sifted through the Rotadex. The Rotadex were seven circular trays which spun in a horizontal axis and which contained index cards of the files contained at P Division. It was all that he had to go on until, as Sussock had said, Computer Services opened for business at 09.00 hours. He stood at the sixth drum, the one containing cards Raeberry to Turvey. He yawned uncontrollably. This was his first night shift in a run of night shifts. Always the killer. It wasn't too bad once your rhythm had adjusted to sleeping during the day and working at night, but the first one, when you were having to work and your body and mind were screaming to sleep, was a killer. It was especially difficult if the work involved tedium and concentration, work like sifting through the Rotadex cards. It was especially bad if he had made the mistake of drinking before coming on duty, or as in this case during the early part of the shift.

He just shouldn't have had those gins. He looked around the room. The collator's desk was empty, the computer monitor was switched off and looked not dissimilar to a blank TV screen, which in fact it was. Overhead lights shone, each filament tube being encased in transparent Perspex to cut out 'shimmer' and so prevent the triggering of a few epileptic fits and not a few headaches. Still 'Stein' wasn't so bad, he'd known occasions when he had been tired enough to sleep on a bed of nails and at the same time had had to look up a 'Smith' or a 'Brown' in the Rotadex.

Eventually he found a card. By luck if nothing else. The card – Stein, Rudolph – had been transposed behind the card on Steiner, Agnes. Tiredness had led to carelessness, which in turn had caused him to move two cards instead of one and so he had found the card he was looking for. Had he been less tired he would have flicked each card until he reached 'Steiner, Agnes,' and then assumed, not unreasonably, that P Division at least had no record of anybody by the name of Stein. But here it was in his hand, a card naming one Rudolph Stein, aged 57, with a smart address in Bearsden, where streams ripple through the front gardens and trees line the driveways full of Volvos and Saabs and Audis, and sometimes the occasional Rolls-Royce. Behind the houses are vast gardens for the pedigree hounds to gambol in.

Montgomerie noted the file number and slipped the card back into its correct alphabetical place. He went to the records room. The room was lined with grey Scottish Office issue filing cabinets, four drawers to a cabinet. A second bank of cabinets positioned back to back stood in the centre of the room. A desk stood by the door. There was nothing on the desk, no chair stood before it, it was just a desk, a small working surface on four legs, with a drawer on the left-hand side. The desk had been brought into the records office long before Montgomerie had joined the CID by two officers who decided that the records room needed a flat surface at about waist height on which a file might be laid, opened and read by two officers standing side by side. So these two officers, legend has it they were named Donoghue and Sussock, purloined the desk which lay behind the uniform bar. The action had taken place in the dead of the night and the uniform bar only discovered the theft after the desk was in the possession of the CID, in place in the records room, and weighed down by a mountain of files. Legend also has it that the item of furniture in question, definitely not of official issue, had in turn been purloined by the uniform bar from a place unknown, probably an interview room. It had been in the building of P Division for some time and the date carved on the front of the drawer, 1929, only three years after the police station had been opened, spoke of the desk's antiquity. The uncertain ownership of the desk probably accounted for the fact that the uniformed boys never launched the expected retaliatory raid to recover possession of the prize, and eventually cobwebs began to grow round the bottom of the legs. At 03.45 on April 2nd, Montgomerie laid the file of Rudolph Stein on the desktop.

Phil Hamilton walked up Maryhill Road from St George's Cross. It was 03.45 A.M. There was the sound of his rubber-soled boots on the pavement, marking the preferred walking pace of two miles an hour. Occasionally he heard a car in the distance, nearer at hand cats screamed and howled at each other for a few seconds and then fell silent.

He wanted a cigarette.

He glanced at the waste ground in front and to the left of him, where about twenty-four hours earlier he had walked, hoping for a discreet smoke, and had in the event discovered a mutilated corpse. In the light from the sodium lamps he could see the orange tape, which marked the location where the body had been found, swinging in the breeze.

Hamilton walked on and wondered how he could have missed them, whoever they were, coming out of the entrance to Wilton Street, carrying the headless body, and the head of the body, and sheet. How many were there? At least two, he thought. One man could carry the body in a fireman's lift, a second could carry the head and the sheet. In all likelihood there would be more than two, unless there had been one, just one man who made the two journeys? Whoever it was had calmly laid the body out, sat the head on the chest, and disappeared silently into the night. Then he, perhaps just ten minutes later, perhaps just thirty seconds later, had walked down Maryhill Road, reached Queen's Cross and had felt the need for a smoke.

Hamilton was a beat cop. He'd walked in the city's streets at dead of night long enough to know that the city doesn't really sleep. If it does sleep, the slumbering bitch sleeps with one eye open and she can rise up screaming and clawing at the slightest provocation.

It's like that in Glasgow at night. Each night, every night. All the time.

There's always somebody about. There's always lights on in some houses, young men revving up motorbikes which they have pushed up the stairs to third-floor flats, loud music played late into the night by unemployed youngsters who sleep away the day, the suspicious meetings where the cops always arrive too late, the all-night buses, the refuse collectors who prefer night working, the insomniacs who can't sleep and go out for a walk and don't at all mind being stopped and questioned by the cops, being glad of the opportunity to talk to someone. Then at about five A.M. the milk boys come out, walking singly or in groups, schoolboys who help out with a milk round before school starts. When the milk boys come out the city's about to open the other eye.

Yet a group of people carried a headless corpse along a street and out into the middle of an expanse of waste ground and left it there. And nobody saw them. The incident occurred right in the middle of his beat and that, he told himself, if he was to be at all honest, caused him more embarrassment than curiosity.

He noticed a movement on the skyline.

Then it was gone. He stopped and searched with his eyes, scanning the towpath.

Yes. There. Running. Running this way, from his right to his left. On the canal towpath.

It was the same figure that he had seen the previous night, just after he had discovered the headless man, except that now the figure was running in the opposite direction. Yes, it was the same figure, hunched shoulders, short jerky movements.

'Two-four-six, control.' Hamilton gripped the radio which was clipped to the inside of his left lapel.

'Control. Go ahead two-four-six.' The female voice crackled on his radio, wavering. The message was in danger of breaking up.

'Code 21. Mobile to intercept suspicious person at towpath and Firhill Street. Over.'

The female voice crackled unintelligibly, swamped by static. Calling Code 21 was, he realized, pushing it a bit. Code 21, officer in need of urgent assistance, was probably more appropriately used when a lone cop was surrounded by club-wielding neds. But he did need assistance, the figure was probably a witness to the murder and 21 was a distinct sound which might get through the static. Then he heard the operator say distinctly, 'Understood.'

Her message broke up. His evidently had not.

Hamilton quickened his pace. He crossed Maryhill Road, and walked up Fruin Street: small shops, locked and boarded up for the night, a funeral parlour, a garage, and, as if to prove an early point he had been making to himself, a light in a first-floor window from which music was playing, loudly.

He was surprised he hadn't had a complaint about the music. Maybe the occupant of the flat was the top cat on the stair, if not the street. Nobody complains about the top cat. It's like that sometimes. On one occasion Hamilton had come across a situation where a man was drawing his electricity supply from two of his neighbours' meters, cables ran to his house from the flat above and the flat below and the man was burning electricity as though it was going out of fashion. 'No, sir, we don't want to complain,' said the neighbours, 'we're happy as it is, very happy.' There's some injustice that the police just don't or can't get access to.

'Control. Tango Delta Foxtrot.'

Hamilton heard the female voice crackle loudly on his radio. So too, evidently, did the occupant of the flat because the music was switched off very suddenly. Too suddenly. Hamilton glanced at the close number as he went by. There was something 'iffy' about the way the music was switched off so quickly. It was a flat to keep his eye on, maybe there was a narcotics deal going down.

'Tango Delta Foxtrot. Receiving.'

'Control Tango Delta Foxtrot. Code 21. Towpath

at Firhill Street. Assist apprehension of suspicious person. Over.'

Hamilton quickened his pace until it was just a spit short of a run. If he required assistance then he'd better look as though he was making some effort to help himself. He reached the end of the houses on Fruin Street from where he could look across open ground to where Partick Thistle football ground stood. He smiled as the old joke occurred to him.

'What time does the match start?' asked the supporter on the phone.

'Don't know,' said the official on the other end of the line. 'What time can you get here?'

Then he saw a white Granada with a yellow flash and twin flashing lights on the roof tear up Firhill Street towards the canal.

Tango Delta Foxtrot was responding to the Code 21.

Hamilton continued his rapid pace towards the point where the towpath met Firhill Street, up at the top, by the foundry. He knew that this could be a significant development in the inquiry. It had to be the same figure which he had seen scurrying away from the locus of the incident just twenty-four hours ago, the same figure for which a panda car had searched the area of St George's and the Round Toll without success. This was too much to be a coincidence. He pressed on, excited.

When Hamilton reached Tango Delta Foxtrot, he saw the car sitting by the side of the road, the engine idling. He approached it from the rear and saw a third person, a member of the public, sitting on the rear seat. Tango Delta Foxtrot had made the pinch. He flashed his torch in the side mirror to signal his approach. It doesn't do to come suddenly upon a cop at 4.00 A.M. The driver wound down the window as Hamilton approached. He was smoking a cigarette.

'Meet Clarissa,' said the driver. 'Subject of your Code 21.' Hamilton crouched on his haunches so that his head and shoulders were level with the head and shoulders of the driver. He glanced at the occupant of the rear seat.

She had fine silver hair, puffy complexion, mottled skin on her forehead. She wore only a thin nightdress and, it later transpired, carpet slippers.

Hamilton glanced at the driver. The driver and his partner were working hard to suppress a fit of hysterics. Eventually the driver said, 'Glad you're the one who's going to have to live this down. Code 21 for a little old lady.'

Then he and the co-driver erupted until tears streamed down their faces.

Minutes later, when they had calmed, Hamilton said, 'Temperature's close to zero.'

The driver nodded. 'Not the collar you expected?'

Hamilton shook his head. 'I thought it might be someone in connection with the incident last night.'

'Hardly think so,' said the driver, still giggling slightly. 'Mind you, it's a good piece of work, just the same.'

'It is?'

'It's the sort of thing the Police Community Relations boys love, to say nothing of the favour you've done Clarissa. Clarissa's looking for her children,' the driver explained.

Clarissa smiled at Phil Hamilton.

'They're seven and nine years old,' said the driver. 'Their supper's on the table and her man will be back from work in half an hour and he'll want his supper as soon as he comes in.'

'Oh hey!' said Hamilton, and pushed his cap backwards on his head.

'Fortunately we know where Clarissa lives,' said the driver. 'She has her address on her key-ring. It's a good example of knowing when you've got to break the rules. Jump in and we'll take you home with her. It's your beat, you may as well know where she stays. You'll likely be seeing more of her.'

Hamilton sat in the rear seat of the car, next to Clarissa. He copied her surname, McIntyre, and her address into his notebook. The crew of Tango Delta Foxtrot dogged their nails and threw the butts into the street and then drove to the address on Clarissa McIntyre's key-ring.

The address was in St George's, a small flat in a low-rise block underneath the shadow of three huge high-rises. The cops located the flat with 'McIntyre' on the door and opened it with the keys. The elderly lady, seeming suddenly to recognize where she was, ran into her home and into her bedroom. The cops followed her in. It was a ground-floor flat, the window in the living room was opened.

'The window's been turned,' said Hamilton. But the room was too neat. Nothing had been disturbed.

'No, it hasn't,' said the cop who had been driving Tango Delta Foxtrot. 'That's how she got out. Mind you, she's been lucky not to have visitors, right enough.'

There was a knock at the door. A middle-aged lady stood on the threshold. She was dressed in nightwear, but had sensibly wrapped herself in a dressing-gown. She looked worried and then relieved as she saw the cops. 'That Clarissa away again?' she said.

'Aye,' said Hamilton. 'We found her on the canal bank.'

'It's a pure sin, so it is,' said the woman, walking into the hallway. 'She in her bed now, aye?'

'Aye.'

'That'll be her for the rest of the night now,' said the bustling woman. 'She never seems to go out more than once a night. It's a pure sin, so it is.'

'Is there nobody to look after her?' asked Hamilton. The woman shook her head. 'She's apparently not bad enough to be taken into a home, she has a home help visit her seven days a week, but that's about all.'

'Does she have family?'

'Two grown-up children. She's a great-grandmother is our Clarissa. Her man's been dead these twenty-five years. She thinks she's living in her tenement and waiting on her bairns to come in from the shipyards.'

'She said she was looking for her children,' said Hamilton, opening his notepad.

'Aye, she would. Did she climb out of the window again?'

'Looks like it,' said Hamilton. 'It was wide open when we came in. Can I have your name, please?'

'Mrs Douglas, Betty Douglas. I stay up the stair from Clarissa. I didn't hear her go out or I'd have been down the stair after her, but I heard you turn the key just now. To be honest, I thought it was Clarissa just about to go away again, she uses the door sometimes, so I was pleased when I saw it was you. But something will need to be done.'

Montgomerie walked quickly up the stairs to the CID corridor. He clutched his notepad. He turned along the corridor to Sussock's office.

Sussock sat at his desk. Montgomerie thought he looked worried, more drawn than usual. He tapped on Sussock's office door and walked in. 'Sarge?' he said. Sussock looked up.

'Stein,' said Montgomerie, tapping his pad. 'Just looked him up as you suggested. Got a record all right, long as your arm, same man, there's a mug shot in the file, he looks like a pear, same guy all right.'

'Indeed?' Sussock was not enthusiastic.

'Long as your arm, well, three prosecutions, fraud, embezzlement, and the like. But the indication on file is that the three prosecutions are just the tip of the iceberg. I bet this guy is one of the biggest crooks in Glasgow.'

'That right?' said Sussock.

'Something wrong, Sarge?'

Sussock patted the phone. 'Senior Fire Officer has just phoned about the restaurant fire in Clarkston.'

'Oh yes?'

'Yes. Point one is that there is already clear evidence of wilful fire-raising.'

'Arson?'

'Is the expression favoured by the English, so I believe. But I'm a conservative Scot, and wilful fire-raising is good enough for me.'

'Yes, Sarge.'

'They have found the charred remains of a timing device, apparently. The Fire Brigade have been trying to contact the owner, but he's not answering the phone. The gentleman has an address in Maryhill and they wonder if we could knock him up. The owner, according to the Fire Brigade's copy of the Business Registry, is a gentleman called Lurinski. One Samuel Lurinski.'

Montgomerie sank on to the chair which stood in front of Sussock's desk. 'Well, well, well,' he said. 'Well, well, well.'

Chapter Seven

Tuesday, April 2nd, 08.30–12.30 hours.

At the shift handover, Donoghue was clean-shaven, fresh, well-dressed, and was beginning to fill his first pipe of the day. Sussock, by contrast, was feeling tacky, he was tired, his clothes were crumpled, he wanted bed. He watched Donoghue fill his pipe and knew that he would be surrounded by a permanent fug for the remainder of the day. Just watching the motion of the man filling his pipe caused a sharp pain in Sussock's chest; it was a legacy of spending years as a smoker. His bronchitis was still always particularly bad in the winter months; now in April the weather was a little warmer, but he wouldn't really be free of the sharp knifing sensations beneath his ribcage until May was out. Then there would be the three months of summer and a pain-free chest. Come October it would start all over again. Scotland is no place for people with bronchial trouble: Like the advert for the sports car says: 'Grips like a Scottish winter, goes like a Scottish summer.'

Sussock had seen Donoghue arriving, swinging his Rover smoothly into the car park at the rear of the police station at 08.28, signing in and collecting any messages from his pigeonhole by 08.29 and at his desk, coat and homburg hung up, at 08.30. Sussock gathered the papers that had accumulated on his desk overnight and walked down the corridor. He tapped at Donoghue's door, waited a full fifteen seconds before he heard Donoghue say 'Come in.' He opened the door and entered Donoghue's office.

'Good morning, sir.'

'Good morning, Ray.'

'Good journey in, sir?' Sussock approached Donoghue's desk, papers under his arm.

'Not bad, bit of a blockage near the Harthill Services, but no real hold-up. Take a seat, please, how's the night been?'

'Enough to keep us busy, but we were not run off our feet. We've known busier.'

'I'll say.' Donoghue clearly remembered the night that off-duty officers were summoned from their beds, himself included. It was the night of a full moon during the white nights of high summer and the city went off her head. It was nothing co-ordinated, just incident after incident, involving one or two people, some felons, some family disturbances, some individuals having complete mental breakdowns, nothing premeditated, but the phones just didn't stop ringing and the cops just hadn't got enough manpower to respond to all the calls. It went on like that until 07.30, when it all went quiet.

'Just a few items to pass on to the CID day shift, sir.' Sussock settled into the chair as Donoghue lit his pipe. 'The first is an attack on a young woman, happened in the night and she staggered into the casualty department of the G.R.I. She'll have to be interviewed by a WPC, but it'll come our way eventually. We know no details except that it was a severe assault, according to the doctor who reported it; she has a name, Louisa Salisbury, and an address in the Tailor's Court Development. She's thought to be in her mid-twenties.'

'You didn't interview her in the night, Ray?'

'No, sir. The doctor said he was going to sedate her to help her come out of shock. He indicated that she would be able to be interviewed later today.'

'Which WPCs are on day shift?'

'Elka Willems for one.'

Donoghue grunted. 'I'll ask her to take a trip down to the G.R.I. and see this woman. What's next?'

'Well, next are two developments in the Lurinski case.'

'Oh good, I like progress.'

'I'm not sure that it is progress, sir. It's more like steaming into an ever thickening fogbank. Montgomerie and King went to the Zambesi Club.'

'Yes, the book of matches. And?'

'Turns out the owner is one Rudolph Stein. He did not at all appreciate the boys visiting him, got ratty in fact. Montgomerie . . .'

'Stein . . .' Donoghue pulled on his pipe. 'We know him.'

'You're ahead of me, sir.' Sussock smiled. 'As I was about to say, Montgomerie looked up the Rotadex in the night: he has a file all right, white collar stuff, fraud, embezzlement and the like.'

'If he's the guy I'm thinking of, then it's him that we failed to nail on an insurance fraud charge.' Donoghue's pipe went out and he lit it with a flourish of his gold-plated lighter. 'About eighteen months ago, I think, he walked when his brief won an argument on a legal technicality.'

'It's not the only one we failed to get, or so Montgomerie thinks. He thinks the three convictions are just the tip of the iceberg. The book of matches is significant. They are not apparently distributed willy-nilly to all and sundry, they have a restricted circulation as it were, just given to Stein's business partners.'

'So,' said Donoghue, 'if they are tied in very closely with Stein, it means there is a good chance that Stein might have given them to the person who was to burn Lurinski's clothing. The fogbank is not getting thicker, Ray. It's dissipating.'

'Well, we're still a long way from linking Stein to the murder, but the boys' visit to Stein definitely worried him. They both had the impression that he had something to hide.'

'Oh good,' said Donoghue. 'I'd be inclined to lean on him a bit more. I'll see what we can do today.'

'Just for your information, sir, King visited Lurinski's employer.'

'He had a busy shift.'

'He came back with a picture of a moralistic, industrious bachelor in his middle years. Came to his work, did his work very well, went home to the house he grew up in. Parents were Wee Frees, apparently didn't like modern conveniences, explains why the house is unaltered. He just kept it as it was. The inside of the house hasn't changed much since he took his first steps.'

'Took his first steps in that house and forty-odd years later he took his last steps in that house.'

'According to King, the only passion Lurinski ever exhibited was strong anti-racist sentiments at the time Royal Exchange Square was renamed Nelson Mandela Place in order to score a point over the South African Consulate which has its offices there. That links in with Lurinski taking a hotel room for a weekend for himself and a lady of oriental background.'

'The Saltcoats connection.'

'That's the one. Abernethy's report will make the point that all indications are that it was not a cheap liaison. Mr Lurinski and the oriental lady seemed to be very close indeed.'

'How interesting.'

'The final thing I have to pass over is an incident of wilful fire-raising.'

'Not another.'

'There's been more, sir?' Sussock coughed. It eased the pain.

Donoghue still puffed and blew and as he spoke smoke came out with the words. 'Well, hasn't there. One a year for the last five years. Never enough to say it's the work of the same team, but the smell is there.'

'I really hadn't made that connection.'

'So that's another investigation to be mounted. Do we have the Chief Fire Officer's report?'

'Not at present, sir,' said Sussock. 'But the CFO believes the fire to have been started deliberately.'

'Premises?'

'A restaurant in Clarkston.'

'Casualties?'

'None.'

'Good. Who have we got that can pick that up?'

'We probably don't need to pick it up as a separate case, sir.'

'We don't?'

'Not when I tell you who the owner of the property is. Or was.'

'Go on. Surprise me.'

So Sussock surprised him.

'We moved her to Ruchill,' said the doctor.

Elka Willems looked at the young man. She thought that she had never seen anyone look as tired as this man looked.

'Infectious diseases ward,' the doctor elaborated in his rich Highland accent which, like Sussock in the night, put Elka Willems in mind of Chief Superintendent Findlater.

'Ah,' said the WPC. 'You were the admitting physician, sir?'

'Yes, last night, back of midnight, perhaps thirty minutes after midnight. She came in, staggered up to the desk, seemed to have sustained a serious assault, bruising, lacerations, the works. She had to wait until we had patched up some car accident victims who were bleeding over everything. I think she had broken ribs in two places. I bandaged them, but that's all, they didn't require resetting and ribs provide their own splints. Otherwise it was just bruising. Well, I'm sorry I said, "just", the bruising was massive, over sixty per cent of her body area.'

'Good grief.'

'Yes, that gave us the first indication that all might not be well. We're getting good at looking for signs these days, the "pointers" as we call them. The bruising, the extent of the bruising . . .' The doctor sat on a wooden chair and Elka Willems rested her notepad and handbag on the leather examination couch. The curtains at the entrance of the examination bay were open and she saw a woman being wheeled past on a trolley. The woman's head was swathed in bandages.

'Look at that,' said Dr Monroe. 'And it's still only Tuesday morning.'

'What time do you get off?'

'This afternoon. I'm on duty for twenty-four hours. I was hoping to snatch some sleep, but no luck so far.'

Elka Willems smiled. 'You were talking about "pointers"?'

'Ah yes.' Dr Monroe shook his head to rid himself of sleep. 'The extent of the bruising was such that I would have expected more fractures than we found, and I would have expected internal bleeding, but again tests for that proved negative. It meant that she had a skin disorder or a blood disorder. There is a condition where, for example, you just have to touch the skin to cause bruising, it's a temporary condition, but quite alarming for the sufferer. I thought she might have something like that.'

'Did she?'

'Would that that were the only problem! Then I noticed other things, thinning hair, localized sores, loose fingernails, patches of raised hard skin. I put her into isolation and sent a sample of her blood to the lab for immediate testing. The results came back at six-thirty this morning. The HIV III test was positive. Very positive. Her condition is very advanced.'

'Condition?'

'She's got AIDS. Acquired Immune Deficiency Syndrome. Her body has no natural resistance to disease or illness and won't recover easily from damage of the sort she's sustained.'

'Oh dear, poor girl.'

Dr Monroe nodded. 'I'm afraid that all she's got in front of her is a very painful death.'

'What sort of time has she got left?'

'The staff at Ruchill will be better at answering that than I am, but, well, we're into April, I don't think she'll see the autumn. This will be her last summer in the world and it will be one summer she'll never have wanted to live.'

'Is it safe to talk with her, Doctor?'

'Yes, you can talk to her. AIDS is infectious, it's particularly, though not wholly, sexually transmitted, but as a generalization, beware of her body fluids. Much, though, depends on her attitude.'

'To me as a cop?'

'To you as a human being who hasn't got AIDS.'

Dr Monroe yawned. 'Excuse me. AIDS sufferers adopt different attitudes. Some are unselfish and responsible and cooperate fully in isolating the virus. Others, fortunately a minority, adopt the attitude of "Well, if I'm going to die of AIDS then I'm going to take as many as I can with me." They have nothing to lose and get a kick out of spreading the virus. They sleep with as many people as possible: one more person infected, one more point to be added to the total score. Unbelievably spiteful.'

'You're not kidding.'

'Edinburgh is the AIDS centre of the UK, more AIDS victims per capita in Edinburgh than in any other population centre, mainly because of the druggies. I was talking to a doctor who works for the Lothian and Border Health Authority, he was telling me of one guy, a heroin addict, who walked into different hospitals around Edinburgh having slashed his wrists, and apparently the blood was pumping out. So naturally the medics and paramedics just dropped everything and stitched him up. When he was patched up and they were covered in his blood, only then did he tell them he had AIDS.'

'The animal.'

'Certainly is. They're on to him now, but he's done the damage and because of him there's not a few nurses and porters and ambulance crewmen and doctors in the Lothians who don't know whether they've got AIDS. All it needed was a drop of his blood to get into their mouths or on to a graze on their skin, or for one of them to prick himself with the stitching needle, and the virus is transmitted.

They don't know whether it's safe to sleep with their marriage partner, and nobody who was involved with this guy will know for certain that they haven't caught the virus for seven years.'

'As long as that?'

'Yes, the body can develop antibodies within three weeks of infection, but the virus can stay dormant for seven years.'

'But you'll be carrying it all that time.'

'That's it. Think what that, as you describe him, that animal has done: those medical staff who stitched him together, working feverishly to save his life, now dare not continue to consummate their marriages with all the problems that will cause. Imagine being a nurse in your mid-twenties who wants to find a husband and settle down and now you can't do so until you're pushing your mid-thirties, and meanwhile lay off sex.'

'How horrible.'

He glanced at his watch. She did the same. It was ten A.M.

'She'll be coming out of sedation by now,' said Dr Monroe. 'She'll have been told where she is and why. You'll be her first visitor and I'm not sure I envy you. She might be hysterical, she might be withdrawn. If she's hysterical and starts spitting at you, just clear the pitch and come back another day. She won't be going anywhere. Do the same if she's happy.'

'Happy?'

'Happy. It's not unusual. People who have broken their spine will say things like "This is the best thing that's ever happened to me, because it's forced me to change my outlook on life," or some other such nonsense. All they are doing is burying their feelings and not accepting reality. If she's like that you won't get anything of value from her. You'll have to wait until reality sinks in.'

'I see.'

'You can talk to her as close as you are talking to me. Just avoid the transmission of body fluids. Not that I think in the circumstances you will be exchanging body fluids, but it's to give you an indication of where the danger lies.'

'Her house?' Elka Willems thought suddenly. 'We may have to go there, what then?'

'Well, if she has a sex partner of either sex, assume that that person is infected, and if you can, persuade them to present at the G.R.I. for tests. Otherwise treat hypodermic syringes, razor blades, broken glass that may have cut skin, anything which might have punctured or nicked the skin, with utmost respect and caution.'

The woman pulled her car to a stop. Normally she would drive up and park outside the restaurant so that she could keep her eye on her car during her working day, and throughout the evening when the restaurant was busy. But today, this bright Tuesday morning in the spring, she could not get within a hundred yards of her place of work. The traffic, normally two lanes flowing in either direction, crawled past in two opposing single files, the drivers and passengers gaping at the still smouldering shell of the building. There were still two fire appliances in attendance, still a single stream of water from a fixed hose playing into the embers. Orange cones sat in the kerb prohibiting parking within a hundred yards of the building. The woman parked her car as close as she could to the building and walked to the barrier which was strung across the pavement. She stood there patiently, and since no fireman approached her, slipped under the barrier and walked to where three of them, serge uniforms, yellow helmets, and axes in heir belts, stood in a group. They carried yellow jackets on their arms. They looked tired and grimy.

'Excuse me,' she said.

'Yes, ma'am,' one fireman said.

'What happened here, please?'

The fireman looked at the short, slender, oriental girl with long black hair. He would have thought it perfectly obvious what had happened, but he was able to be diplomatic. 'We don't know, madam, that is to say the cause has still to be established.'

'When did it happen?'

Just now, madam. It happened just now, in fact it is still happening, you see those bits of wood that are glowing red, they are called embers, and you see that jet of water there which is pumping hundreds of gallons a minute into the embers, that is called a fire hose, and it's like that because . . . but.

'We think it started about midnight, madam.'

'But nobody was hurt?'

'We don't think so. If you'd move along now, please?'

'But I work there. It's my business.'

'Oh, I see. Can you wait a moment.' The fireman walked to where another group of firemen were. He spoke to a Fire Officer with a blue peaked cap. Then the officer with the peaked cap glanced at the woman and approached her.

'You work here, madam?'

'Yes,' she said. 'I am the manageress.'

'We tried to contact the owner during the night, a Mr Lurinski, I believe, but he didn't answer the phone.'

'That's strange.' The woman looked questioningly at the Fire Officer. 'He was at home over the weekend and also last night, at his old home, I mean. What number did you try, please?'

'I don't have a note of it, madam, but it was a Maryhill address. G20, I think.'

'That would be his address. He certainly will be at work at the moment. He works in Nelson Mandela Place, perhaps you could contact him there?'

'Perhaps. I wonder if you'd like to come and sit in the car, madam?' The Fire Officer guided her by the arm. 'The police will probably want to interview you.'

'The police? Why?' The woman allowed herself to be led towards the red car with the blue revolving light on the roof.

'Just routine.' The Fire Officer opened the door of the car for the woman. Inside the car he radioed to his control. Could they please telephone P Division

Police, ask for DS Sussock in respect of the Clarkston fire. The manageress of the restaurant had arrived on the scene. Did they wish to speak to her.

Donoghue took the call. 'DS Sussock is off duty, may I help? Yes, I see, yes, I'll send a car to escort her over to us. Thank you.'

The manageress of the restaurant was escorted to P Division by two constables in an area car. In the police station she was shown to an interview room and asked to take a seat. She sat in the room and looked about her, a table against the wall, two chairs at either side of the table, a hardwearing carpet on the floor. A tape-recording machine on a shelf. The walls were painted yellow. The door was varnished wood with a small pane of reinforced glass set in it at shoulder height. She noticed that the door could be locked if necessary.

She wondered what stories these walls had heard.

She wondered why Samuel Lurinski had not answered the phone during the night.

She wondered why the police were so anxious to talk to her that they had escorted her to this police station north of the water.

She became worried. A terrible worm of doubt and suspicion began to grow inside her.

The door opened. A tall, slim man entered. He had a thin yet fleshy face with short, well-groomed dark hair. He wore a three-piece charcoal grey suit and a gold watch chain looping across his chest. He wore a white shirt and a university tie. She thought him to be in his early forties. He carried a pipe and a tobacco pouch in his right hand. 'Good morning,' he said, warmly. 'My name is Detective-Inspector Donoghue.'

She stood up.

'Oh, please sit down.' He saw the look of worry in her eyes and wished that he could say, 'Look, there's nothing to worry about.' He doubted that he would be able to say that. He thought the girl was in her early twenties. She had a smooth pale yellow complexion, long dark straight hair. She wore high heels, but, even wearing them, stood less than five feet six inches tall, or so it seemed.

She sat down. He sat opposite her and opened his notepad.

'I gather you are the manageress of the Bay Leaf Restaurant in Clarkston, which was destroyed by fire during the night?'

'I am,' she said.

'The fire came as a surprise to you? I mean, I assume you didn't read about it in the first edition of the *Herald* or the *Record*, or hear about it on the news?'

The woman shook her head. 'I read only the *Evening Times*,' she said, 'and I don't have opportunity to listen to the radio.'

'I see. Could I take a note of your name, please?'

'Chi Chu Lurinski,' she said.

Donoghue echoed, 'Lurinski?'

The girl nodded, pride spilling over, especially as she repeated her surname for Donoghue's edification.

* * *

Malcolm Montgomerie awoke and swore softly. Without looking at his watch he knew he had slept little. He had signed off at 09.00 hours, had got home in a rapid fifteen minutes, crawled thankfully into his pit at 09.30 hours and now what time was it? He reached out and scrabbled on the surface of the bedside cabinet for his watch. He brought it towards him and groaned as he read the time. Just ten after twelve. Not even three hours' sleep.

Outside he could hear the traffic growling along Highburgh Road. He heard the children yelling in the yard of the nearby school. Perhaps it was they who had wakened him. Whatever it was, he was awake now and he knew he would not sleep again, unless he happened to doze off while sitting in the armchair as he soaked up television prior to going to work again at 22.00 hours.

He closed his eyes and tried to fight off the sense of resentment he felt when woken early, the sense of resentment at having been cheated of sleep. He opened his eyes again and looked around his room. The curtains were drawn, but the thin material could not shut out the light. He looked around his room at his clothes strewn everywhere, left where they fell as he had flung them off just a few hours ago.

A drawer opened and shut in the kitchen. A plate was taken down from the shelf and placed noisily on the working surface.

So that was why he had woken. She had come home for lunch. He imagined that she thought she was being silent. He levered himself up and swivelled out from under the duvet and pulled on his dressing-gown. He went into the kitchen.

Michelle turned round once and looked at him, then she looked away. 'You look a mess.' She wrestled with a can of sweetcorn.

'And you woke me up,' he growled. 'I asked you to keep quiet, you know I'm on night shift.'

'I was quiet.' She rattled the saucepan on the cooker as she emptied the sweetcorn into it. 'I left the radio off. But since you're awake . . .' She extended an arm and pressed a button.

Rock music assaulted Montgomerie's ears. He walked forward and pressed the same button.

Silence.

'Leave it off,' he said. 'It's too early.'

'It's after midday.' She opened a drawer and slammed it shut. She wasn't in a temper, but every movement was accompanied with a flourish and a drawer could not be opened without also moving it from side to side or shut without being slammed home.

'It's too early for me.'

'Malcolm . . .'

'Just leave it off, will you?'

'You're selfish.'

'Maybe, but it is my home and not yours. Just leave it off.'

He went into the bathroom and stood under a warm shower. Then he braved a cold one, then turned it warm again. The girl, he thought, was all bustle as maybe fits a gym teacher, but she was immature and insensitive. He shampooed his hair. She was looking like one of his shorter liaisons, but she had provided yet another scalp to hang on his belt. Time to hunt new thighs, Malcolm.

Chapter Eight

Tuesday, 2nd April, 13.00–15.00 hours.

In the event it was both easier and also more harrowing than Elka Willems had anticipated. It was easier because of the attitude of Louisa Salisbury, and more harrowing because she was quite unprepared for what she saw.

The AIDS ward she found to have a chilling severity, a silence which was not at all oppressive, a ward like most hospital wards, with rows of beds, and in each bed lay an adult female quietly contemplating an early death. Elka Willems thought the ward staff seemed to be more considerate, caring, and sensitive in their approach than their counterparts on the general wards. Although this, after all, was terminal care; no malingerers here. The ward had a smell of diarrhoea which permeated the smell of disinfectant. She was to be told that there was an outbreak of diarrhoea in the ward, it was difficult to control, and just one more infection that the body cannot fight. As in any AIDS ward, once an infection takes hold it is difficult to combat. The men's ward was rife with dysentery.

As she stood and waited for the screen to be drawn around Louisa Salisbury's bed she could not help herself looking with horrific fascination at the patient in the adjacent bed. The patient was drained of all colour, her cheeks were hollow, the eyes had sunk in their sockets, her flesh was covered with a rash, her hair was falling out. Her arms were thin and her hands clawed like a bird's leg and foot, she lay back, staring at the ceiling drawing each painful breath with a harsh, rasping sound.

'She's twenty-eight,' said Louisa Salisbury as Elka Willems sat beside her bed. 'We were talking before you came, only she can't talk much before she starts hurting. She'll go deaf and demented. Then she'll die. She told me that she knows that because she's seen others die, the one ahead of her in the queue, like she's ahead of me. So I'll watch her die and then I'll know what I'm in for. I wish they'd have us in little cubicles instead of open wards. I've found out already that you just want to be alone with your thoughts.'

Elka Willems smiled at the young woman. It was a sincere smile of compassion and acknowledgement of the woman's evident courage. Louisa Salisbury responded by smiling back and then paid Elka Willems the ultimate compliment of one woman to another. 'You are very beautiful.'

'Thank you.' Elka Willems took out her notepad.

'Do you have Scandinavian blood? You don't look Scottish somehow.'

'My father is Dutch,' said Elka Willems. 'My mother is a blonde-haired Fifer. She says she is of Viking descent. I dare say Scandinavian blood runs strongly through my veins. I am Scottish, though. From Stranraer.'

'I was pretty once. It was nice,' Louisa said reflectively. 'Do you know why I'm here?'

Elka Willems nodded.

'Doesn't it frighten you?'

'No.'

'You're very brave.'

'Not at all. It's a lot less dangerous for me here than it is on my beat. Sometimes I get scared when I'm on my beat. I don't always go with a partner, there's just me and my radio and my torch, trying doors and shining the beam up alleys and closes, checking any noises.'

'I didn't think WPCs went out alone at night.'

'Yes, we do.' She took a pen and began to scribble on her notepad. 'It's not so dangerous. It's really very unlikely that someone will leap out at you. Gratuitous violence like that is very rare. Most of the time you can see trouble developing and all you need is ten seconds to press the send button of your radio and say "Code 21, junction of Argyle and Nairn," and within sixty seconds there will be half a dozen police cars and "jeeps" on the scene.'

'Jeeps?'

'It's what we call the large vans we use. Still, despite that I do get scared at times, but it's often just my own imagination that is giving me things to be frightened of. In reality there is little to be scared of. A couple of cats scream and knock over a can and your heart leaps a beat because you immediately think someone is being done in. Mind you, in your case I guess it wasn't just a couple of cats.'

'Which is why you are here.'

'Yes.'

'You're not so far off, it wasn't cats, but it was a couple of animals all right.'

'Tell me.'

But the woman paused. Elka Willems felt a sense of disappointment. She had felt that the woman was going to be cooperative and was unprepared for the resistance to her questions. She felt she had to keep the sick girl talking. She knew that she wasn't going to get anywhere by interrogation, but it was important to keep the dialogue going. It was Elka Willem's experience that some people will tell you what you want to hear if you nibble around the edges of the issue, while others will let you go straight to the heart of the matter. Elka Willems felt that this girl would only allow her to nibble.

'Do you know how you caught the disease?'

'Let's call it AIDS, shall we,' said Louisa Salisbury. 'We both know what's happening here. Yes, I know. I was a smack head.'

'Heroin?'

'Smack, horse, H, heroin, a rose by any other name . . .'

'OK. You can tell me the name of your pusher later.'

'He gave me the disease,' she said. 'Maybe a year ago, it's been incubating inside me all this time. I've passed it on to at least one other person.'

'Did you inject, use other people's works, I mean?'

'No.' Louisa Salisbury shook her head. 'I smoked it.'

'I see.'

'Gave up.'

'You make it sound easy. That's unusual.'

'It is easy.'

'I know it is,' said Elka Willems.

'Why, have you been there yourself?'

'No. In service training. They told us that addiction to heroin is hysterical not physiological. It's still a strong addiction, especially since it's group hysteria, but it's hysteria all the same. Did you come off it easily?'

Louisa Salisbury nodded. 'Stomach cramps for a couple of days. Nothing to complain about. I got out when I realized just how much it was dominating my life. I was nothing but a smack head. Stealing for the next fix. Unbelievable, really. Even went on the game.'

'Is that how you got enough money for a flat in the Tailor's Court?'

'Oh, you know where I stay.'

Elka Willems nodded. 'You had a letter in your handbag. The hospital staff looked in there because they needed an identity, in case they had to contact your next of kin. You were badly beaten up.'

'I was going to tell you that I stay with my mother in Parkhead. But since you know otherwise . . .'

'Is your mother your next of kin?'

She nodded. 'She doesn't even know I'm here, I wonder . . .'

'Yes,' Elka Willems said. 'I'll tell her, if you give me her address. Do you want me to tell her what your condition is?'

'Could you? I'd appreciate it.'

'Yes. If you want me to.'

'I dare say that I owe you, now?'

'You can start by telling me about your pusher.'

'My ex-pusher. I kicked the dragon. Remember.'

'OK, your ex,' said Elka Willems. 'Tell me about your ex-pusher.'

'Tell me something first. How do you know that it's easy to give up heroin?'

'It's the story of the old lady in Manchester, England, an authenticated case written up in the medical journals. She was diagnosed as suffering from cancer and her GP prescribed daily injections to ease the pain and arranged for district nurses to ensure that she had an injection each day of the week, including public holidays. She never missed a fix every day for fifteen years. The GP subsequently retired. The practice was taken over by a new GP, who realized that there must have been a misdiagnosis. So he went to see the old lady and said that he was sorry the treatment had taken so long, but that she was now cured and he was stopping the injections. He expected her to go through all sorts of horrific withdrawal symptoms.'

'And?'

'Nothing, save a running nose for a couple of days.'

'Really?'

'Really. You see, she never knew that it was heroin she was being injected with, to her it was her "medicine". She was living an addict's dream, but all she had by way of cold turkey was a running nose for two days. So that case and others like it is how we know it's easy to give up heroin. It's harder to give up alcohol and tobacco.'

'I won't be worried about that. I intend to drink myself stupid in the time I've got left.'

'I'd do the same, I think,' said Elka Willems. 'So are you going to tell me who did you over?'

'Two guys. Broke into my flat and gave me a kicking. No sooner were they in than they'd gone. They were good at their job.'

'You didn't recognize them?'

Louisa Salisbury shook her head.

'Any idea why they would do it?'

Again she shook her head, but this time Elka Willems knew she was lying.

'You haven't told me about your pusher?' Keep her talking.

'You know him.'

'We do?'

'He's inside at the moment. Peterhead. He was given five years for possession with intent to supply. Guy by the name of Jamie "Bull" McKee.'

'Doesn't ring any bells with me.'

'He's just a petty ned who got out of his depth. He could do a little crooking and not get caught, then he got greedy and began to make mistakes.

Then he got his collar felt. He got lifted and got the gaol.'

'Tell me the old, old story.'

'Aye, guess there's nothing new in this tale. I always went to him when I needed a fix. I paid cash normally. I got the cash by shoplifting clothes and sold them to a fence for ten per cent of the retail price. Two quid for a twenty pound dress. He'd sell the clothes at the barrows. He still has a stall down there. I needed nearly a hundred quid a day for my smack.'

'Who was the fence?'

Louisa Salisbury paused.

'You're not involved any more. He'll not know who fingered him.'

'Guy called McCourt. Big Sean McCourt, evil bastard. Comes from the Isle of Man.'

'Where's his pitch?'

'Close to the entrance to the Barrows, which is just across the road from the Sarrie Head.'

'I don't think we know him. Just across from the Saracen's Head?'

'Yes.'

'We'll take a look at him. How old is he?'

'Pushing forty. Huge beer belly.'

'Anyway, back to your pusher?'

'Yeah, he was a smack head himself, and he was gay. Well, bisexual. He shot it up with filthy works, rusty needles, all that number. On the occasions I hadn't the cash I used to nip him.'

'Nip him?'

'Sleep with him. I did it quite often. It was cheaper than paying for it, and not at all unpleasant.'

'So you think it was him who gave it to you?'

'He's the only one could have. He slept with as many boys as women and used dirty works to shoot up; the same needle time after time. I went to his flat one time when he and his mates had been shooting up. They had passed the syringe around the group, there was a plastic bucket on the floor full of blood and vomit and blood was splattered up the wall after one of them had opened an artery. Had to be him. All the other guys I've been with have been straight and not druggies.'

'I don't suppose it matters who gave it to you,' said Elka Willems. 'The thing is that you've got it. Mind you, we'll inform Peterhead, they'll get this man, McKee, screened for the virus.'

Louisa Salisbury nodded. 'A death sentence is a death sentence. The judge's I/D is not important.'

Elka Willems glanced out of the window. A young woman was walking round the grounds. Louisa Salisbury saw her looking out of the window.

'Is there a woman walking?'

'Yes.'

'She's got legionaire's disease. Part of the treatment is to get good lungfuls of rarified air. What better air than Scotland in the spring?'

'What indeed? What do you do for a living, Louisa?'

'This and that.'

'Don't give me that. You've got a flat in Tailor's Court, you've got money. You on the game?'

'No.'

'So where does your money come from?'

'I work for the man.'

'As?'

'Personal Assistant.'

'I see. So why didn't you say that instead of giving me the runaround. So what time did they break in?'

'Late. Close on midnight. Maybe a little after. I was just about to go to my bed.'

'They just kicked the door in?'

'Not exactly. I fell for the oldest trick in the book. There was a gentle tap on the door, like a child's knock, I keeked through the peephole. There was no one on the landing. So I opened the door. It was held on the safety-chain, but they kicked it in anyway. These doors are just matchstick. The locks and chains are strong enough, but they are not screwed into strong wood. It's just plywood over a thin frame.'

'And you've no idea why or who would do this?'

'No, I haven't.'

'Come on, Louisa. You've taken a good doing, girl, somebody did it for a reason.'

'Maybe they did. I don't know what it was or what was their reason.'

'I see. So who's your employer?'

The woman paused. Then she said, 'A guy called Stein. Rudolph Stein. He has a number of businesses, bars, discos, restaurants.'

'He'll have a few enemies. Businessmen always do. Perhaps somebody is getting at him through you?'

The girl shook her head. 'That makes no sense. He's not that bothered about his employees. I think it was just a couple of neds who wanted to burgle the flat.'

'Did they steal anything?'

'I really don't know. I left the door open and went up to the Royal . . . the door's still open. Half of Glasgow has probably been in and out by now.'

'Do you want us to secure the premises?'

'Could you?'

'Yes, it's a reasonable request to make of the police, that and also to notify your next of kin. Two things for us to do. Sure you don't know who'd want to give you such a belting?'

'Sure I'm sure. Anyway that's the least of my problems.'

She was stoical at first. She tried hard to fight the tears, did well too, thought Donoghue, but finally broke down. While she was burying her face in a series of Kleenex, Donoghue had plenty of time to take in a wide wedding-ring and an engagement ring with a cluster of diamonds around an emerald. She was a valued lady.

'You were married to Mr Lurinski?' said Donoghue as soon as she seemed ready for a question and answer session.

She nodded.

'Long?'

She shook her head. 'Two weeks.'

'Two weeks,' Donoghue echoed.

'Two weeks married and then widowed,' said Chi

Chu Lurinski. 'You know, we hadn't even begun to live together, we hadn't even gone on our honeymoon. We went to Gretna to get married. You can't do it at the Blacksmith's shop any more, but the registry office there does thriving business. In keeping with the tradition, many couples travel from all parts of the UK to get married at Gretna. They could go anywhere in the UK to get married if it's a civil wedding they want, but there's something about going to Gretna, especially if your romance has an element of rebellion about it. We drove for two hours down the A74 and walked into the registry office and became man and wife. The staff there acted as witnesses.'

'Your romance had an element of rebellion?'

She nodded.

'In what way?'

'In many ways. In fact in every way our romance was pure rebellion. I rebelled against my family who wanted me to marry within the Chinese culture. I couldn't do that, I've been to university, I've become westernized. I couldn't become a subjugated woman. Do you know that it's not uncommon in the Chinese families for the man to keep a stick for the sole purpose of ensuring his wife's continued subjugation? Also he will not allow her to cast a vote at election times.'

'It's not so different from the natives.' Donoghue began to fill his pipe. 'In the West of Scotland a man may beat up his wife if the drink he has consumed immediately prior to the incident is not less than twelve pints of strong lager.'

'I take your point, but the subjugation of women in the Chinese community is more ritualized and integrated into the culture. I really didn't know any other way until I left school. I took a job in a large store and not only did I get treated the same as white women, but I also overheard male trainees getting shouted at for the same mistakes I got shouted at for making. I was being treated the same as a white male. It made me realize that I was something more than a chattel and baby factory.'

'Still, it took some courage to break away from your background.' Donoghue lit his pipe.

'I broke away by going to university. I went to night school for highers and then to the uni. It's the best and easiest way out.'

'So did I. I came from the Saracen.'

'Really. That's a tough district.'

'One of the toughest. I went to the university here in Glasgow,' said Donoghue, 'then joined the police force.'

'I went to Stirling,' said the woman. 'I seized the opportunity to leave home.'

'That's a sensible thing to do. I often regret not going away to study. Did you know that seventy per cent of the students at Glasgow's two universities live with their parents? The figure for English universities averages less then two per cent.'

'I didn't know that.'

'Yes. Scotland follows the European model in which students go to the university in their home town, if there is one; if not, then to the nearest university. In England students move to a different town even if there is a university in their home town. It's apparently a continuation of the English tradition of sending their children away to be educated.'

'How interesting.' But Donoghue could tell that her thoughts were elsewhere, and who could blame her. He thought she must be feeling the void felt by all sudden widows. Where now? Who now? She was younger than many widows, still in her twenties, she was intelligent, she had a strong personality, she seemed to have a certain capital. She had, to an outsider, much to compensate her in widowhood, but it would take time for her to find it. It could only be one day at a time for her for the foreseeable future.

'You were telling me about the rebellion in your marriage?'

'Oh yes. I'm sorry, I was not thinking.'

'Take your time. You were saying that your family didn't approve.'

'No, they didn't, not in principle, but they liked Samuel on a personal level. He had a pleasant, sincere humility about him which we Chinese value. It was especially appealing in a rich white man.'

'So your family wouldn't hurt him?'

'Oh no, no, really, Mr Donoghue, you're not thinking that he was murdered by my family?'

'I'm not thinking anything, Mrs Lurinski, I'm keeping an open mind and I'm exploring every possibility. I have told you that he was murdered with a bladed instrument. I'm afraid that his death was a little more than a stabbing.'

She looked startled. 'You mean he was hacked to death?'

'In a manner of speaking. I'm afraid he was beheaded.'

She covered her face with both hands as she absorbed the shock.

'There is also a further element of ritual involved in your husband's murder,' Donoghue continued as gently as he could, 'in that Mr Lurinski was dressed in clean clothing, not just clean, but new, apart from his suit which was recently drycleaned.'

'His green suit? I took that to the drycleaners' myself, just last week.'

'And his body was carried outside and left on a piece of waste ground, with his head on his chest.'

'Oh, Samuel . . .' She grabbed another tissue. It was some moments before Donoghue felt she was ready to talk.

'I'm sorry to have told you that, Mrs Lurinski, but . . .'

'I would have found out anyway. You're right, I think I'd rather hear it here than in a courtroom.'

'I mention it as well because it has certain similarities to the Sauchiehall Street attack of some months ago.'

'I know the one you mean,' she said. 'The Chinese businessman who wouldn't sell his string of oriental food shops to the Triad. He was thrown out of a taxi in the middle of Sauchiehall Street on a Saturday afternoon, hands and feet cut off.'

'That's the one.'

'Nearest you got, according to the papers, is that

the assault was carried out by Chinese imported from another city, maybe Liverpool, they were illegal immigrants controlled by the mob who'd do anything to avoid being reported to the authorities, get shipped back to Hong Kong and then to mainland China.'

'That's the one. The papers didn't miss anything. We just couldn't penetrate the Chinese community. Talk about silence, they made the Cosa Nostra look like a WRVS knitting bee.'

'And you see similarities: the ritual, the public example, both businessmen, a Chinese element, even the new clothing could be significant.'

'Oh.'

'Yes, the last thing that a Chinese gathers about him or her is four wardrobes of unused clothing.'

'I didn't know that.'

'Yes, one wardrobe for each of the seasons so that they have sufficient clothing for their journey in the next world. They are buried wearing the wardrobe which is appropriate for the time of year in which they die, and the other three wardrobes are placed in the grave, alongside the coffin, sometimes in the coffin, but that isn't always possible here in the West.'

'So the new clothing is an additional Chinese cultural element.'

'Yes, but the similarity between the two incidents is superficial. The Chinese might mutilate another Chinese, but they wouldn't do that to a European unless that European had taken the initiative against them. You see, the Chinese gangs in Garnethill and other parts of the city, but mainly Garnethill, they are basically families with second cousins having the same strength of bonding as brothers in Western families. The families go at each other with machetes and knives and do dreadful damage, but it's strictly confined to the Chinese community; they don't drink so they never run amok. They are always in control and always know who they are going to go up against, but the aggression and violence is never visited upon Westerners. The Chinese are aware that we are a guest race in Glasgow and we go to great lengths to avoid conflict with the whites.'

'But you can take care of yourselves,' said Donoghue. 'I witnessed an incident once where half a dozen Glasgow neds made the mistake of trying to roll two Chinese boys. I've never seen so many bodies fly at the same time. The two Chinese just walked on as though nothing had happened.'

'Yes, we can protect ourselves. But despite my race, Samuel would not have been murdered by any members of the Chinese community. Like I said, they took to him on a personal level, and even if they hadn't, then the fact that he married me made him part of the family.'

'Would it also have made him an enemy of your family's enemies?'

'Yes. But they wouldn't have involved him in that manner. As I said, the Chinese live in fear of a racial conflict with the whites, and Samuel wasn't that big enough an enemy to run such a risk. My family has an enemy family, but to them Samuel was only a token enemy. They knew him, recognized him and ignored him.'

'Thank you.'

'What for?'

'A full and frank answer. It couldn't have been easy for you, but I'm afraid it was an avenue I had to explore.'

'I quite understand.' She reached for another tissue. Donoghue knew that this couldn't be easy for her. She was a strong young woman.

'Can I ask the nature of Mr Lurinski's rebellion?'

She smiled softly. 'It seems strange to talk about rebellion in a middle-aged man, but there was a lot of conflict inside Samuel's head. Do you know his background?'

'Not fully.'

'Well, he was the only son of Free Church parents, both Scottish, the surname came from an Eastern European who settled in Scotland in the nineteenth century. His parents, I never knew them, were very Wee Free, all fire and brimstone, any form of enjoyment is sinful. They kept their house in Maryhill in its original condition, no modern conveniences at all.'

'Yes. I've visited it.'

'Very oppressive.'

'I quite liked it.'

'Well, from a historical point of view I dare say it's interesting, but I didn't like it because I could feel the suppressiveness of the Free Church inside the flat. Samuel rebelled against that too late in life, after the death of both parents, turned his back on the church and that caused him great anguish. Then he started drinking, never let it get hold of him, but he'd take a pint and then go to a nightclub. Can you imagine that, a middle-aged man among a lot of children? After he'd been to a nightclub he'd go into a state of guilt-laden depression. I mean, it was a big thing for him to go into a pub, a nightclub was to dance with the devil.'

'How did you meet?'

'I had a small business, a shop, selling oriental artefacts, silks, kimonos, chopsticks, mah jong sets, that sort of thing. In terms of disposable income I would have been better off in teaching, which was the original idea, but I was my own boss. I liked that. I walked into Samuel's office one day and asked for professional advice with my accounts. We took it from there, though in the early days I had to make all the running.'

'Eventually you got married.'

'Yes, and the manner in which we married was rebellious for Samuel, a civil ceremony and not a church service. That was the final act of rebellion.'

'Had you known each other long?'

'Two years. We became business partners before we became marriage partners.'

'Oh.'

'Yes. We have three Chinese restaurants, all on the south side. One of which was set on fire last night.'

'So Samuel Lurinski was a married man with a business empire?'

'Yes. It was a small empire, but we planned to expand.'

Donoghue re-lit his pipe. He asked amid the puffing and blowing if Samuel Lurinski had any enemies in the business world.

'Not anyone who would want to kill him. I think he would have told me if he had.'

'I see. Can I ask why you were not living together?'

'We did. In my house in Busby. Samuel's wardrobe stands next to mine in the big bedroom. What Samuel did was to keep the house on in Maryhill and he kept going back there, sometimes living there. I think he was putting off telling the cleaning lady that he was selling up and was to be letting her go.'

'To return to your business life, none of your other restaurants have been subject to wilful fire-raising?'

'No. We've never had any problems before today, and now my husband I find to have been murdered, and our newest and best restaurant is deliberately set ablaze. What else can happen? We Chinese believe things happen in threes.'

'So do we.'

'But what can happen? My business is in ruins, literally, my husband is dead . . .'

There was a shuffling footfall in the corridor. Donoghue stood. 'Excuse me,' he said. He opened the door of the interview room. 'Abernethy?'

'Sir?' Abernethy turned suddenly. He was tall, slim, good CID material though still learning, but with his inquiring mind and his ability to worry away at a problem Donoghue was convinced that he would grow into the CID.

'Yesterday morning Ray Sussock told me you were holding the cases of five wilful fire-raisings.'

'Yes, sir.'

'Can you tell me about them, please?'

'Now, sir?'

'Now, sir. This instant, sir.'

'Well, they stretch back over six years, all deliberately started but with varying methods. I'm afraid I haven't got anywhere with them.'

'Or the case?'

'Sorry, sir.'

'Because there was no obvious link doesn't mean to say that they are not connected.'

'Certainly, sir . . .'

'What sort of premises are involved?'

'Nightclub, a sort of café with a liquor licence, two pubs.'

'The sort of places where people go to enjoy themselves?'

'Yes, sir, since you mention it.'

'No factories, warehouses, for example?'

'No, sir.'

'So there is another link besides all of them being fire-bombed.'

'Yes, since you mention it, sir.'

'Location of fires?'

'Shawlands, Pollokshaws, let me see, pub in Priesthill, Langside, two in Langside, and last night's incident in Clarkston.'

'All on the south side of the water.'

'I had noticed that, sir,' stammered Abernethy. 'But I thought it was coincidence.'

'It's not a good idea to jump to conclusions, Abernethy. Assume everything to be significant until proved irrelevant.'

'Yes, sir.'

'I'd like you to dig out some information, please,' said Donoghue. 'Can you find out who is the present owner of all the properties which were fire-bombed?'

'The present owner?'

'Yes. As opposed to the person who owned them at the time of the bombing.'

'Certainly, sir. Will you be here or in your office?'

'My office, please.'

Donoghue returned to the interview room and sat down opposite Chi Chu Lurinski. 'Sorry for that interruption.'

'That's quite all right. I couldn't help overhearing. There've been other arson incidents?'

'Yes, since you overheard. We don't know if they are connected, we're exploring that possibility now. Well, thank you for your cooperation. I'll have a car drive you home.'

'Thank you.'

Donoghue sat in his office. Layers of blue tobacco smoke hung in the room, kept aloft by the central heating system. He was writing up his account of the interview with Chi Chu Lurinski, the upshot of which was that, as previously indicated, there was much more to her husband than met the eye, but his feelings were that Mrs Lurinski was not implicated in her husband's death in any way.

There was a tap at his door. Donoghue laid his pipe in the huge ashtray which he kept on his desk and said, 'Come in.' Abernethy entered. He looked worried, ashen-faced, drained of colour. Donoghue looked at him and raised his eyebrows.

'The properties you asked me to inquire about, sir. They are all owned by the same man. Except for the Clarkston fire yesterday.'

'A man called Rudolph Stein?'

Abernethy's jaw dropped. 'Yes, sir. How did you know?'

Donoghue tapped the Lurinski file. 'A little bit of information here, a copper's nose, intuition, and reasoned assumption. Have you anything on at the moment?'

'No, sir.'

'Good. Grab your coat. You and I will pay a call on Mr Stein, at his home.'

'He probably won't be at home this time of day, sir.'

Donoghue stood and reached for his homburg. 'Oh, good,' he said.

Chapter Nine

Tuesday, 2nd April, 15.00–17.00 hours.

Elka Willems drove from Ruchill Hospital to Tailor's Court. Tailor's Court stood just off Albion Street, a few hundred yards from George Square. Tailor's Court was originally a warehouse, it was bought by property developers, gutted and split into individual flats. Elka Willems saw it as one of the more responsible acts of property development. The Tailor's Court Development kept people living in the centre of the city and so helped to prevent the 'dead heart' syndrome so common in the late twentieth century in cities where the heyday had been in the nineteenth century. And in Glasgow the Tailor's Court Development made a significant contribution to the preservation of the city's vast heritage of Victorian architecture. Elka Willems had grown extraordinarily fond of her adoptive city and could already see that the Victorian architecture of Glasgow, not just individual buildings, but squares and long thoroughfares, was rapidly becoming as prized as the Georgian architecture in the city of Bath.

Elka Willems located Louisa Salisbury's flat on the second floor at the front of the building. The door was still smashed and splintered about the lock and hanging half off its hinges. She reached into her uniform handbag and pulled on her black leather gloves. She knew that they would probably not prevent her from picking up an infection of the deadliest sort, but wearing them made her feel a little more protected.

The flat was smaller than she had imagined, as though the developers had wished to squeeze as many flats as possible into the shell of the old warehouse, but they had not lowered the ceiling so that the flat's walls were abnormally high for the floor size. The decoration was painfully loud to Elka Willems's taste, all yellows, blues and reds. Harsh, very harsh on the eyes. She found the flat superficial in content: books bound in blue leather with titles embossed in gold, ranged behind a glass panel in a bookcase. There for decoration, not to be read. There was a yellow-coloured metal bed on a blue carpet; there was a print of a painting of an angelic-looking child who had a single tear running down his cheek. The furniture in the narrow living-room, with its vaulted ceiling, was disturbed, out of place, the coffee table was upturned, and the 19-inch television screen had been kicked in. There was a splattering of blood on the sofa and on the walls. She had been beaten up here. Elka Willems, as advised, treated the blood 'with respect'. She checked out the bathroom; there was blood in the bath and in the wash-hand basin, blood on the facecloth and on the mirror. The girl had staggered in here bleeding badly and had attempted to clean herself up, before walking up to the hospital. The blood had dried, but even in its dry state was still teeming with AIDS virus. Elka Willems backed gingerly out of the bathroom.

She went back to the bedroom. The double bed took up a large proportion of the floor space. Most of what remained was taken up by a wardrobe, a chest of drawers, and a dressing-table. There was just enough space to walk alongside the bed between it and the items of furniture. She had heard of the practice among some modern housing developers of decorating their show houses with scaled-down furniture. She could well believe the rumour to be true, going by the rooms in Tailor's Court.

She opened the drawers of the dressing-table, reverently sifted through another woman's most personal possessions. She was looking for a notebook, a letter, an address book, anything.

She heard keys turn in the lock.

She looked around.

A door opened and shut. Feet marched across the ceiling, a hi-fi was switched on and the music beat loudly downwards filling Louisa Salisbury's flat. The folk upstairs had come home. Elka Willems returned to the living-room. A small bureau stood in the corner. It was of an old design with a roll-down top, but it was modern, made of heavily stained chipboard, and not as large as an original writing bureau would have been. It was light in weight and Elka Willems opened it delicately, afraid of breaking it. It was as fragile as a toy. She despaired of people who reached deep into the purse to possess such items of furniture.

There was an address book inside the bureau. She looked through it. There were just two entries. Louisa Salisbury's mother and a man called Rudolph Stein. She copied Stein's address and phone numbers, his office number and his home number. She left the flat and coaxed the door shut behind her.

She drove out to Parkhead. Low-rise tenements, dull, grey, narrow streets off London Road, small overgrown gardens full of litter, spray-painted graffiti: 'Screw the polis', '1690', 'Fenian Drummie'. Mrs Salisbury had a two-room-and-kitchen, ground-floor left. The door with 'Salisbury' on the front was deeply scratched and chipped and daubed with paint. The lock and the frame and the plaster around the frame had been splintered. The door had once been forced open, though not in recent weeks. It was a vivid insight into the history of the flat.

Elka Willems rapped on the door. There was no response. She knocked again. Then someone inside the flat yelled, 'Who is it?'

'Police,' said Elka Willems, loudly enough for her voice to carry through the door.

Two keys turned, the safety-chain was taken off and Jessie Salisbury opened the door. Jessie Salisbury had a broken nose, missing teeth, matted hair and a grime-encrusted face. She was certainly considerably younger than she looked. 'Aye?' she said.

'Mrs Salisbury?' Behind the woman Elka Willems could see a darkened corridor and walls of naked plaster.

'Aye.'

'Can I come in for a minute or two? It's about Louisa.'

'Louisa. She in trouble, aye?'

'Yes. But not with the police.'

'Trouble? You'd better come in.' The woman stepped aside and allowed Elka Willems to enter the flat. She followed Elka Willems down the corridor which smelled heavily of damp, and into the living-room.

The living-room smelled musty. The carpet had been trodden into a soft mass so that the pile had congealed with the underlay. The settee was old and greasy, as was the chair in which Mrs Salisbury was evidently sitting, and in which she now sat, moving round the tall policewoman in a hunched, shambling manner.

'Take a wee seat, hen,' said the older woman.

Elka Willems was relieved to see a hard-surfaced chair in the corner of the room. She sat on it.

The gas fire was turned up high, there were empty bottles and empty special lager cans on the floor. There was a picture of the Queen on the wall. The curtains were partially closed, the windows were grimy. She looked out of the window on to a waste land behind the tenements, where one brave woman had hung out her washing over the rusty bike frames. One pane of glass in the Salisburys' flat had been put in and the hole had been covered with black plastic taken from a bin-liner and Sellotaped on to the frame. The plastic blew in and out like a bellows as the wind scoured the backs. The interview with Mrs Salisbury was to be punctuated by the continuous flip-flap of the plastic and the hiss of the gas flame.

'We've been having a wee drink since Saturday,' said the woman. 'Me and my man.' She glanced at the floor underneath the window and Elka Willems suddenly realized there was a man lying there, he was lying face away from her and dressed in an oily boiler suit. The black hair, the dark clothing and the utter stillness of the man succeeded in camouflaging him in the gloom. 'Aye, he can sink a good bucket, can Jamie,' said the woman, smiling with pride. 'Would you like a wee goldie, hen?' The woman reached for a bottle of whisky and an empty glass.

'No, thank you,' said Elka Willems. 'Duty.'

'Duty, I see,' said the woman. 'Will you take a coffee? I'll see if there's a clean jar. We had some jam pieces yesterday, we finished the jam. I can give it a good wash and give you a coffee. No?'

'No, thanks,' said Elka Willems, beginning to feel itchy.

'So it's about Louisa?'

'She's in hospital.'

'Oh, in the name of God! Serious?'

'Yes, I'm afraid so.'

'Which one?'

'Ruchill.'

'I'll need to get up there. I can tap money for a taxi.'

'I'd sober up first,' said Elka Willems.

'You think I'm drunk?'

'Yes.'

The woman sat back in her chair. 'Aye, well,

maybe I am. Maybe I am a wee bit. See, me and my man have been on a wee bender since Saturday.'

'One day won't make much difference,' said Elka Willems. 'I'm sure she'd rather see you sober.'

'It's not that serious, then?'

'Yes. It's serious. But it's chronic rather than critical. She can wait until you're dried out, so long as you stop drinking now and get your head down.'

'Well, that's all right, then. I'll go tomorrow.'

'Louisa grew up here?'

'Aye. Till she left.'

'Sudden as that.'

'Aye, one day she was here, one day she wasn't. She left about four years ago. She doesn't call and see her ma at all.'

'Does she see her father?'

'Never knew who he was, hen.'

'I see.'

'Do you? See, me and my men, it's been like being a pit terrier all my days. My man he put an axe over my head.' She ran her fingers through her hair. 'My scalp's like a pocket full of zip fasteners, the scars have been stitched together, five of them. Put me in hospital, so he did, he got five years. He'll be out soon. See Jamie there.' She nodded at the still mound on the floor. 'See him, he doesn't know about my man, and my man doesn't know about Jamie. I've got a wee problem there, so I have.'

'I think you have.'

'You sure you don't want a wee drink, hen? I've got a bit of lemonade, could make you a nippy sweetie.'

'No, thanks.'

'See, my man he wrote me a letter. See, that letter, it was the only letter I ever got from a man. He'd just got the gaol and he sent me a letter. Know what it said?'

'Tell me.'

'It said, "Gonny see my gear's stashed right. Kenny." That's all. He just got the gaol and he wrote me wanting his clothes put away right, he's got a jacket with a velvet collar that no one gets to touch. That's how I know he's coming back to me.'

'Did you see it was put away right? Other women would have flung it out.'

'Not me, hen. I stand by my man, and I wouldn't want another doing. See, Jamie, he can give me a right doing when the fancy takes him, but he doesn't use an axe. He's got to be away before Kenny gets out, otherwise Kenny'll take an axe to me again.'

'How long have you got?'

'He gets out next week, Kenny does.'

'Better get something worked out.'

'Aye.' She poured herself another whisky. 'Aye, I'll work something out, aye. I'll need to. Ruchill, you say.'

'Ruchill.'

Outside, someone had poured acid over the bonnet of Elka Willems's car.

'It's made of glass fibre.'

The voice came from behind Donoghue and Abernethy. Both cops turned. The owner of the voice was a thin, drawn woman in her middle years.

Abernethy was startled by her waiflike appearance and Donoghue thought: Internal growth. She swayed on her feet. She had auburn hair, cut untidily short, she wore a green dress and red shoes. 'Just glass fibre.' Her voice was slurred.

Both cops sighed with disappointment.

'It doesn't look like it, does it?' she insisted. 'But it's just glass fibre.'

'No.' Donoghue turned and glanced sideways at the Buddha, four feet tall, sitting cross-legged with arms gently outstretched. It glistened in a darker green than the green of the dress of the alcoholic female who had told them it was made of fibreglass. Donoghue took a pace forward and tapped one of the arms of the figure. Fibreglass it was, but it was an exceptionally skilful piece of glassing and painting. He had thought it jade.

The Stein household was on Duntocher Road, Bearsden. There was the road, the pavement, mature hawthorn hedgerows, gravel driveways, sunken lawns, then a bridge which spanned a stream, not any trickling brook, but a fully fledged torrent which was just shy of being a river and which cut all the front gardens on one side of Duntocher Road in half. Then there were the houses, squat in appearance but bigger than they looked, and behind the houses were alpine gardens. Donoghue and Abernethy walked up the driveway of the Stein household, across the bridge, and turned right towards the front of the house. Then they came face to face with a Buddha.

'My husband is the man who loves the Orient,'

said the woman. She held out her hand. 'I'm Mrs Stein.'

Donoghue shook her hand and then she extended it towards Abernethy. She gave both cops the strong impression that her gesture was born out of starvation of tactile contact, rather than a desire to be well-mannered. 'Touch hunger,' the psychologists call it.

'Is Mr Stein at home?' asked Donoghue.

'No.' The woman swayed gently like a sapling in a breeze. 'He's at his offices.'

Dongohue savoured the old Glasgow expression for place of work.

'Can I help you, gentlemen?'

'Perhaps.'

'You are?'

'Police.' Donoghue showed her his I/D. Abernethy reached for his. Mrs Stein shook her head at Abernethy. 'It's all right, young man. If one is the genuine article, I'm sure the other is. Shall we go inside? It's chilly out here.'

The interior of the house was spartan, spare of furniture, yet managed to exude a feeling of wealth. The floor was wood, highly polished, with a lambskin in the centre. Cushions lay on the floor instead, Donoghue presumed, of chairs. A vase with reeds stood in the corner, a low coffee table stood in front of the firegrate. The windows were covered with paper blinds. Two ornamental swords in their sheaths hung side by side on the wall. A second Buddha, smaller than the one outside the house, stood in the corner opposite the vase and reeds. The original doors had been removed and lightly framed partitions covered with rice paper stood in their place. The light bulb hung from the ceiling extending close to the floor and was surrounded by a round paper lantern cover. The house was silent. It had a fragile feel, as if music would be destructive. Mrs Stein stood in the centre of the room holding her shoes in her hands.

Donoghue and Abernethy had no intentions of removing their footwear.

'Some coffee, gentlemen?'

'No, thank you,' said Donoghue with a kind firmness. He felt that the offer of coffee, like the extending of her hand, was born out of some personal desperation rather than it was Mrs Stein playing the lady of the house.

Mrs Stein walked unsteadily across the floor and placed her shoes near the back door of the house. She returned to where Donoghue and Abernethy stood. 'Is it my husband you wish to see? Oh, you just said that and I said he was at his offices.'

'Just you and your husband live here, Mrs Stein?'

The woman nodded. 'Just him and me. Me and him. I'm here all day and night and he's just here some of the time. When the fancy takes him he's here.'

'I see.'

'Do you?' The woman screwed up her eyes to focus on Donoghue, as if trying to clear her head of alcohol. 'You are a policeman. I dare say you see life in your job, maybe more than most. Is it not fairly obvious to you what I am?'

'You have something of a drink problem.'

The woman smiled. 'The only drink problem I've got is that I can't get enough of it. I drink to think. I've got a lot to drink about. A drink problem? Why don't you just say alcoholic like everyone else. Frankly, I didn't know policemen could muster such diplomacy.'

'So you're an alcoholic,' said Donoghue. 'If you like. Now where does that get us?'

'I wasn't always an alcoholic.'

'I should hope not.'

'My husband made me an alcoholic.'

'He drove you to drink?'

'Not in that sense.' The woman rocked backwards and forwards. 'More in the sense of actively encouraging my drinking, it pleased him to see me drinking. So I pleased him. I mean, what would any wife do? He knew what he was doing all right. He knew fine well what he was doing. The drink got me in the end, it had to, and now I've got my wee planks about the house. What do you think I was doing in the garage when you came up the drive? It's vodka in the garage, the bottle's in the coal bucket underneath a lot of old newspapers. I've got a bottle of rum outside next to the water barrel. It's only the heavy bevvy I take. Nothing else, just heavy bevvy. You know, I haven't bought a bottle in three years. My husband keeps all my planks topped up. We play a daft wee game, he puts another bottle in place when the last one's getting empty and I drink it and we kid on we don't know what the other one is doing. How to murder your wife without actually killing her. He's fiendish clever all right.'

'You could get out if you've a mind,' said Donoghue. 'There's de-tox programmes available.'

'It's not so easy. I'm trapped. You can't start a de-tox programme unless you are sober when you enter the hospital. If I begin to look sober he just pours me a drink. You know, when he's here he brings me my morning cup of tea and there's always whisky in it, just to make sure I get off on the right foot, just to make sure I start the day right. Then I eat, I can only eat in the morning, a slice of toast, an egg, by ten I'm usually moroculous drunk, too smashed to hold anything down. I've got no money and little strength, I can just make it to the garage and back. I haven't been beyond the drive for years. Do you think I'm happy? Do you think I like this? You're going to say I could leave him, but who'd sleep with a wasted old bag who reeks of booze, who'd take me in off the street, and all the while there's the promise that the next glass will hold the answer. What do you want to see my husband about?'

'We hoped he could help us with our inquiries.'

'That's a lovely phrase.' Mrs Stein swallowed involuntarily. 'I love that phrase when I hear it on the news. "A man has been detained in connection with the incident and is assisting police with inquiries." Lovely.'

'What is the nature of your husband's work?'

The woman smiled vacantly and shrugged her shoulders. 'He has a number of interests, but only one main one. That's the Orient. Anything to do with China, see what he's done to my house, made it like the inside of a pagoda. He's got costumes as well. Used to have me wear a kimono, now he just gives me a bottle and shoves me away in a room.'

'I meant business interests,' Donoghue pressed her.

'I'm out of touch. I've been kept out of touch. I became an embarrassment. He kept me out of the way. I think he met a floozie, he hasn't made any demands – you know, demands – for some time. My husband comes home two or three times a week, picks up the mail, makes sure my bottles are topped up. Sometimes he comes and goes in a couple of minutes.' The woman swayed. 'At least it seems like a matter of minutes. It could be hours. I'm getting to have difficulty telling the passage of time. Will I tell him you called?'

As they walked away from the house, their shoes crunching the gravel, Donoghue said, 'She hadn't a clue who we were and when she wakes up tomorrow she will have no recollection of our visit.'

They drove into Glasgow and went to the Zambesi. It was just beginning to fill with the drink-on-the-way-home-from-work punters. One or two of whom would doubtless still be there at throwing out time.

'Police.' Donoghue flashed his I/D at the young man with the white shirt who was wiping the wooden gantry top with a damp cloth. 'We'd like to see Mr Stein.'

'Downstairs, sir.'

Donoghue and Abernethy went back outside and

down the alley, beneath the level of the pavement, which ran alongside the building. The metal door at the end of the alley was shut. Donoghue knocked on it. He knocked again, impatiently. Then it was opened. A well-built young man said, 'We're shut.'

'I know,' said Donoghue. 'Police. To see Mr Stein.'

'I'll see if he's available.' The man began to pull the door closed. Donoghue grabbed it and pulled it open.

'He's available,' said Donoghue. He and Abernethy followed the man into the gloom.

Stein was sitting at the bar, leafing through a ledger. Donoghue was shocked at just how grotesquely overweight Stein was, and he wondered at the strength of the pedestal of the bar stool that could support such a heavy man. Stein wasn't wearing a jacket and his silk shirt clearly revealed fat hanging around his waist, drooping over the belt of his trousers.

'I couldn't stop them at the door, Mr Stein,' the young man pleaded as Stein turned.

'Stop who?'

'He couldn't stop the police.' Donoghue held up his I/D for Stein's edification.

'Again. I had a couple of your boys visit me yesterday, last night in fact. I don't like cops on the premises. It makes the place look bad.'

'Quicker you talk, quicker we'll go on our way. Is there somewhere we can talk?'

Stein nodded to the tables and chairs beside the dance floor, all at present empty, the chairs leaning against the tables. 'It's as good a place as any.'

They sat down. Stein leaned forward. Donoghue reclined slightly but by no means in total supplication. Abernethy sat upright but moved his chair furthest away from the table. The interview was to be between Donoghue and Stein, he was there to observe.

'Mind if I smoke?' Donoghue took out his pipe.

'Be my guest. Won't make any difference in this atmosphere anyway.'

Donoghue looked up and could clearly see smoke from the previous night's revelries still hanging in the air, picked out by the dim glow of bulbs near the gantry.

'I can't get a half-decent extractor fan,' said Stein, by means of explanation. 'Soon as it breaks I get it fixed, soon as it's fixed it breaks. How can I help you?'

'We're still pursuing inquiries into the death of one Samuel Lurinski,' said Donoghue. Then he stopped speaking to light his pipe, but studied and enjoyed the look of alarm that flashed across Stein's eyes, and the look of indignation growing on Stein's face, sharply picked out in the gloom by the flickering flame of Donoghue's lighter. 'A booklet of Zambesi Club matches was found near his clothing, the indication being that they were used in an attempt to burn the clothing.'

'So I believe. Anybody could have taken them from here.'

'That's not quite true, is it? The matches are not handed out to the public. They are of limited supply.'

'Not that limited.'

'No?'

'No.' A hard edge crept into Stein's voice.

'I understand you have a number of other business interests besides this one, Mr Stein?'

'That's no secret.'

'Restaurants, bars, discotheques . . .'

'Is there a law against it?'

'Mostly bought cheaply following fires.'

It was at that point that Stein gripped the table and said no more questions unless his solicitor was present. Donoghue was not at all displeased with the progress he had made.

In the car driving back to P Division through the grid system, along Bath Street, up over the summit and down to Charing Cross, Abernethy asked what was the point of the interview, sir? Had it not only succeeded in giving him advance warning, time to prepare a defence? Fix up an alibi?

Donoghue drummed his fingers on the steering-wheel. 'I think we succeeded in putting him on edge, hopefully he might trip himself up. Most of all I just wanted to meet him, he had succeeded in intriguing me. I'm convinced that not only is he behind the murder of Lurinski, but he's also one of the biggest crooks in Glasgow and we're only just learning about him. He's been carrying on like this for years and heaven only knows how many extortions, arsons, murders, are down to that guy. All we need to do now is nail him.'

'Where now, sir?'

'Wherever he leads us.' Donoghue drove into the car park at the rear of P Division police station.

'Sir?'

'I'd like you to get an unmarked car and drive it back to the Zambesi Club. Sit in it and stay in it. Follow Stein when he emerges. If you're still there at 17.00 hours, I'll have Dick King relieve you.'

Chapter Ten

Tuesday, April 2nd, 17.00–23.30 hours.

It was Richard King who tailed Stein. King arrived at P Division at 17.00 hours, spoke briefly to Donoghue and then drove into the city to relieve Abernethy at, according to the notebooks of both officers, 17.21. King sat in the unmarked car from 17.21 until 19.33 watching the rush hour as much as he watched the entrance to the Zambesi Club.

Stein emerged at 19.33. He walked heavily, a huge raincoat draped about him. He went a short distance along the pavement to where a Mercedes Benz was parked. Stein clambered into the driving seat of the Mercedes and joined the traffic stream. King wound up the Ford and nudged in behind the Mercedes.

Stein drove over the Kingston Bridge and out to Busby. As King followed Stein, keeping a respectable distance behind him, he began to feel a dull foreboding, a sinking feeling, a feeling of disappointment mixed with anger. He was beginning to develop the sort of intuition that Donoghue had honed to perfection. As he drove out along Clarkston Road, where the architecture is pleasantly solid and suburban rather than tenemental, past the shell of the burnt-out restaurant, he expected with growing certainty that Rudolph Stein was going to call at, as the police jargon would say, the house of Lurinski.

He was not disappointed.

Stein pulled up outside the house, pumped the horn twice and Mrs Lurinski, dressed fetchingly in black, left her house and walked up to the Mercedes and got into the front passenger seat.

DONOGHUE: Taking Mrs Lurinski out to dinner?

KING: Yes, sir, at the casino, they played a couple of games of roulette and blackjack, lost money and then went upstairs to the restaurant. They're sitting up there now.

DONOGHUE: You're in the casino?

KING: Yes, at the pay phone near the entrance.

DONOGHUE: Careful not to let them see you. She went willingly with him? No sign of coercion?

KING: None that I could detect. She came out to his car quite willingly and was tarted up to the nines.

DONOGHUE: Still alone in her house, no one else there?

KING: No. That's the other thing I have to tell you, as I drove past her house, just following Stein and Mrs Lurinski as they drove off, the house lights were on and the curtains open.

DONOGHUE: And?

KING: House full of Chinese guys, sir. That is to say, at least half a dozen gentlemen of oriental extraction. I saw a couple of small suitcases on the table, the sort of size somebody would take for an overnight. They were standing in the room talking.

DONOGHUE: Curiouser and curiouser. Relatives up for the funeral, perhaps?

KING: Who knows?

DONOGHUE: Who indeed. I don't think there's any point in you hanging around any longer, Richard, come back in, there's something else to be done. I think I shall call and see Mrs Lurinski later on this evening, or maybe tomorrow. I think it's time we started to lean on a few people.

KING: Very good, sir.

Both cops replaced their phones at exactly the same moment.

Donoghue reached for his pipe and cradled it in his hands. He looked at King and then at Elka Willems.

'Well, as I said on the phone, it's high time we started leaning on a few people. We've been sniffing around long enough and we're not moving in any particular direction and I'm afraid of losing the impetus, even if the inquiry is still only two days old. As I see it, there are two people to put under pressure. Both females.'

'Not Stein, sir?'

Donoghue shook his head. 'As I said earlier today, I'm quite convinced that Stein is at the bottom of all this. I believe he was attempting to take over Lurinski's business empire. As always, the problem is proving it. I think if we lean on Stein he'll just scream for his lawyer. The way I see it is to approach

Stein through the two females in his life, the luckless Louisa Salisbury and, so it would appear, the other lady, Chi Chu Lurinski, mourning widow of Samuel Lurinski. It'll mean working late for you, Elka.'

'No problem, sir.'

'Back again?' Louisa Salisbury levered herself up as the nurse drew a screen around her bed. The effort of movement caused her obvious pain and King was distressed to see her condition. He saw the heavy red rash over most of her face, her fingers were bandaged at the tips. Her arms, so far as he was able to see, were also covered with the same rash. Her hair was thinning. 'It's bad tonight,' she said. 'Bad chest pains. They bandaged my fingertips to stop the nails falling off.'

'We'll not detain you any longer than we have to,' said Elka Willems, but thought how, just how in the name of humanity, can you 'lean on' someone in this condition. Donoghue just doesn't know what he's asking us to do.

King stood behind Elka Willems and was still taking in the awful stillness and quiet of the ward and noticing how the strong smell of disinfectant could not suppress the all-pervading smell of diarrhoea.

'I don't mind talking,' the girl said. 'It doesn't hurt to talk. I'm glad of the company. I get depressed just lying here thinking about death. I'm only twenty-three. I'm not ready to die. Life just can't be so cruel.'

Elka Willems reached out and took Louisa Salisbury's hand.

'That's brave of you,' said Louisa Salisbury. 'You must be about the same age as me.'

'I am,' said Elka Willems. 'More or less, just a little older.' She sat by the bed.

'You get some respite with illness,' said Louisa Salisbury. 'It's a bit like being on a swing, up and down, but each time you go up you never go as far as you did the last time, and when you go down you go down further each time. One of the girls died this afternoon, just after you left in fact. They wheeled her out in a concealment trolley. As soon as she died they put her in a plastic bag, clear plastic which is sealed to make it completely airtight. The relatives view the body like that, through a sheet of Cellophane. She'll be cremated. It's not compulsory, but they ask you to agree to it. The nights are worse. You just lie and think and try to sleep as pain shoots through your body and you look at the clock and twenty minutes has gone by since you looked at the clock the last time.'

Richard King thought she was a very brave young woman.

'It's all happened so suddenly. Two days ago I was walking around the city, feeling sick, feeling tired, but basically OK; now here I am and I know I won't leave this ward except in a plastic bag. Did you see my mother?'

'Yes. I told her where you are. She'll come and see you.'

'Did she have a good drink in her?'

'Yes,' said Elka Willems. 'But she took in what I told her all right.'

'Like mother, like daughter,' said Louisa Salisbury. 'We both get a right doing off a man and end up in hospital. Some guy chopped her up with a hatchet.'

'So she told me.'

'He got the gaol for it. He'll be coming out soon and see if she doesn't take him back, she'll take him back all right. I think she feels safe with a man who knocks her about, daft as it sounds. There is a sense of security that some women feel if their man gives them a good kicking. I don't feel like that myself but I can see how some women can feel that way. Even if it involves a hatchet. She'll see it as being her fault for annoying him. Anyway, you haven't called to see me without a reason, no?'

'Yes, we've a reason,' said Elka Willems. 'See, we think you know a bit more than you're telling. You're a shrewd lassie and you obviously know that the more you talk the more you control an interview and the more you can shift the discussion away from the less comfortable areas.'

'There's no fooling you.'

'I've been a cop for too long, Louisa.'

'Death bed confession is it?' She looked at the ceiling, high and white. 'Dare say I've nothing to lose, dare say I won't be around by the time he's brought to trial.'

'Who's brought to trial?'

'Stein. That's who you are talking about, isn't it?'

'Yes.'

'Aye. I thought so. See, the plans I had, the places I was going to visit. We all have an ambition, something we want to do. I wanted to go to Canada, to see the Rockies and the Great Lakes. I've been promising myself that trip for years.'

'You're moving away from the issue again.' Elka Willems smiled but her voice was firm.

'Stein,' said Louisa Salisbury. 'He topped that guy Lurinski. I saw it.'

'That's all we want to know,' said King. 'Do you mind if I take some notes?' He took his notepad out of his pocket and took the tip off his ballpoint.

'See, Stein's been trying to buy out Lurinski for some time. Lurinski wasn't having any of it, possibly it had something to do with the fact that Stein was offering peanuts instead of money. Lurinski just wouldn't budge. So Stein decided to burn him out.'

'Like he did the others?' King asked.

'You know about them as well?'

'Yes.' King nodded. 'You can give us the details later, we'll just talk about the Lurinski murder for the time being.'

'Well, first thing you have to know is that Stein is obsessed by the Orient, anything oriental is OK with him.'

'So we gather,' said King. 'My boss visited his home.'

'You remember that incident some months ago, a Chinese guy wouldn't sell out to the Chinese Mafia, the Triad or Tong or something, they cut his hands and feet off and threw him out of a car in Sauchiehall Street one Saturday afternoon?'

'I remember,' said King. 'We got nowhere with that case. Most we ever knew was that a Chinese hit team were imported. They did the business and left.'

'Well, that incident set Stein to thinking. He said, "See those Chinese guys, that's the way to do it. We'll knock off Lurinski and then put a proposition to his co-owner." She's a Chinese lady by coincidence.'

'She's also his wife.'

Louisa Salisbury looked shocked. 'Stein didn't know that.'

'I dare say he'll find out soon enough. So what's your part in this?'

'Me, I'm his moll, his bit of stuff, and his driver when he needs one. He held his council of war at Tailor's Court.'

'Your flat?'

'He's the owner, but I live there.'

'So, because of your relationship we can assume that Stein is infected as you are.'

'Yes,' said Louisa Salisbury. 'Go carefully as you arrest him. No violence if possible, don't cut him.'

'We'll go carefully.'

'So that's how I found out where and why he intended to murder Lurinski. He decided we should call on Lurinski, him and me and Spike and Castlemilk Fats.'

'The two guys who work upstairs at the Zambesi?'

'The very same.'

'One's a student, so he told us.'

'Is he hell a student! That'll be Castlemilk Fats,

he works hard at the image, but in fact he's hardly literate. He's a vicious, evil thug. They took me along because they'd all taken drink to give them courage and I was sober. They needed me to drive the motor. Stein has this massive Mercedes. Top of the range number.'

'I've seen it,' said King.

'So we went up to Maryhill and more or less pushed our way into Lurinski's house and we found ourselves in the dining-room. Stein was mad, I don't mean angry or out of control, I mean mad, pure insane. He was as cold as ice. If Lurinski had said, "OK, I'll sell out for your offer," it wouldn't have done him any good. Stein had decided Lurinski was going to be topped and nothing was going to stop him. It's the way Stein's mind works.'

'So what happened?'

'They started talking. Lurinski got a bit more relaxed. Spike and Castlemilk Fats were talking to Lurinski. Stein moved behind him. He had a sword under his coat, a Japanese samurai sword. It's an imitation, but it's sharp enough. He keeps it in his house. He has two, I think, but both as sharp as a razor. Anyway, when Lurinski was looking away Stein brought out the sword, held it with both hands and swung at the back of Lurinski's neck. I've never seen anything like it.'

'I should hope not,' said Elka Willems.

'Lurinski's head just fell forward but not off the shoulders, it was still attached by some skin, the blood just shot up like a geyser and then Lurinski's body fell forward.'

'Why the clean clothes?'

'Stein's bampot idea. He thought it would help us get away with it, in case we got fibres from his clothing on ourselves or vice versa. We guessed at the sizes and got a suit from the wardrobe in his bedroom. It's not easy dressing a corpse, and there's an odd musty smell that comes from them like dried leaves. We were all wearing gloves, rubber washing-up gloves. Stein insisted we wash the body. I don't know why, he was just agitated and illogical but we had to soap him down and cleanse him with industrial alcohol. Stein had a bottle. He said it was the right thing to do. Since we killed him we had to clean him up, then dress him in new clothes. He thought it would help us cover our trails.'

'Then what?'

'We waited. See, we filled him in at about midnight, there was still a lot of people about, so we waited until about two or three in the morning.'

'You carried him all the way from his house to the waste ground?'

Louisa Salisbury shook her head. 'No, we carried him to the motor, drove the motor to the side of the waste ground, carried him out, body first, head and sheet second. They went home, I dropped them off where they stayed and left the Mercedes in the centre of town at a pre-arranged place so Stein could pick it up later in the day. I was to burn Lurinski's clothes. They'd been parcelled up in brown paper. I took them to a demolition site south of the water. I tried to burn them, I couldn't – the rain, you see. So I left them, I was feeling ill, so I walked home.'

'You walked?'

'I looked for a taxi. I couldn't see one. Eventually I was so close to Tailor's Court that it was just not worth hailing a cab.'

'Then?'

'Later in the day Spike and Castlemilk Fats kicked my door in and then kicked me in. Stein had found out that I'd fouled up the burning of the clothes. So I took a good kicking and was warned to keep my mouth shut. So I have nothing to lose, nothing to thank Stein for. If you want hard evidence against Stein there'll be blood on the rear seat of his flash motor and maybe on one of his swords.'

'Thanks,' said King. 'Thanks a lot.'

'I feel better for telling you that,' said Louisa Salisbury. 'Never intended to get involved with the likes of Stein, but once in it's impossible to get out.'

'You getting tired?' Elka Willems asked.

Louisa Salisbury nodded. 'Come and see me tomorrow and I'll tell you what I know about Stein burning out businesses to force the owner to sell to him. To put it simply, he picked business premises which were part of a string of businesses owned by the same man, all to do with entertainment. He torched one and then went to see the overall owner, made sure there was no witnesses and said, "That's one, I can do the others as well and even make it look as though you set it alight yourself so there's no guaranteed insurance payment, or you can sell to me for my price."' Louisa Salisbury looked at the cops. 'I may as well do something useful with my time, such that I've got left, and turning supergrass is as good as anything.'

Again King found himself thinking that Louisa Salisbury was a brave woman. Then he telephoned Donoghue from the ward sister's office.

'King, sir.' he said. 'At Ruchill. We've got enough for a warrant for Stein's arrest. We'll also have to seize his car for Forensic to go over. There's likely to be Lurinski's blood on the rear seat.'

'I see.'

'Also there is apparently a samurai type sword in Stein's house, possibly two.'

'There are two, I've seen them.'

'Well, one is the murder weapon and may still have traces of Lurinski's blood on the blade.'

'Good.'

'You'll need to advise the arresting officers to handle Stein with care. Louisa Salisbury is his mistress. It means that Stein is carrying the AIDS virus. If he resists arrest and starts fighting his blood could fly. Could be dodgy.'

'Thanks. I'll make sure that that information is circulated. We'll go up to his house later on tonight, give him time to take Mrs Lurinski home. If he's not there we'll visit Mrs Lurinski to see if Stein's an overnight guest.'

King put the phone down. 'Thank you,' he said.

'Welcome,' said the ward sister.

'Tell me,' said King, 'Miss Salisbury, how long has she got?'

'Not long, I'm afraid. We're still learning about the virus, but in her case it seems to be racing, galloping along. She's probably in her last three weeks, perhaps a month.'

'As little as that?'

'She's going down rapidly. Things are beginning to fail.'

'I noticed her fingers have been bandaged?'

'The nails are being forced off by a fungus growth in the quick. Between ourselves it won't do any good at all, but it stops her from having to see her own body falling apart and it gives the impression that something is being done. She'll lose bowel and bladder control, her sight may fail and her mind will fail. She'll possibly be demented before she dies.'

At his desk Donoghue began a series of telephone calls. First he dialled an Edinburgh number. His wife answered. Donoghue regretted that he'd be working late tonight and no, he didn't know what time he'd be home. His wife sighed as she always did on such occasions and said that she would leave a casserole in the oven.

Donoghue phoned Montgomerie. A female answered the phone, asked Donoghue to wait and then Montgomerie said, 'Malcolm Montgomerie.'

'Donoghue here, Montgomerie. I'd like you to come in early. We're making arrests in connection with the Lurinski killing.'

'Very good, sir.' Montgomerie put the phone down. He looked at Michelle.

She looked at him, both standing, naked. She moved towards him and nestled against his chest. He said, 'I have to go out.' She leapt as though she had been stung. She stared at him with a look of disbelief, indignation and disgust. 'You can't be serious!' She folded her arms over her breasts. 'Not now, just now, not at a time like this.'

'You took the call, you know it has to be serious.'

'Duty can't come before us.'

'It has to.'

'Why can't you get a daytime job?'

'There'll be other times.'

'Not with me there won't.' She snatched her robe and spun herself into it and stormed out of the room.

'I happen to like my work,' said Montgomerie to a slamming door.

Ray Sussock sat in the chair in the empty room. He nursed a mug of coffee in one hand and sat wearing his hat. It was cold in the small room and he was losing his body heat. In front of him on an orange crate was his black and white TV which had a metal coat-hanger pushed in the back to serve as an aerial. He was tuned into the BBC Scotland because, and only because, it was the best picture he could receive; even then it was heavily snowed with crackle on the sound. He had eaten late, as he tended to do when working the night shift, and now just sat in front of the television, killing time.

The house had quietened. The couple on the floor above had had a screaming, blazing row during which, so far as Sussock could tell, she had been pushed out on the landing and the door locked behind her, whereupon she worked herself up to a hysterical state, banging and kicking on the door.

Eventually her man opened the door, but only to let himself out, rather than her in. He stamped down the stairs and out of the house, presumably to go to the nearest bar. Sussock anticipated round two would start when he returned, full of drink. In the next room the two men who wore their sweaters in their trouser belts and who lived together played music softly. It had been louder earlier on in the evening and he had tapped at their door and asked them to turn it down. They had obliged politely, but had annoyed him by calling him 'dad'.

In the circumstances that was a bit too close to home.

Now the music was still low, but the walls were so thin that the sound still penetrated into his living space. Soon he would have to endure the sickening grunts of their nightly coupling.

The pay phone in the hallway rang. It rang out and kept ringing. Eventually one of the boys relented and went downstairs to answer it. He came bounding back up the stairs and hammered irreverently on Sussock's door. 'Call for you, dad,' he said when Sussock opened the door.

'Sussock,' said Sussock when he reached the phone.

'Donoghue here, Ray. Can you come in early, we're making arrests in the Lurinski case.'

'Delighted,' said Sussock.

'There'll be two arrests simultaneously,' said Donoghue, standing between two desks in the CID room sipping a coffee. In the room listening to him were

King, Montgomerie, Ray Sussock and Elka Willems. All were similarly drinking coffee. 'We'll have good support from the uniformed branch. Montgomerie and King, I'd like you to handle the arrest of the so-called Spike and Castlemilk Fats. The Zambesi shuts at 01.00 hours, that's in about ninety minutes,' he said, glancing at his watch. 'So we'll make that zero hour. We'll let them get their last shift in. Remember, don't underestimate these two, they're part of a vicious murder, don't be taken in by that student earning an honest penny in his spare time garbage.'

'Very good, sir,' said King.

'Now, should Stein be there, huckle him in as well, radio to us and we'll meet you here, back at the station. But I'm presuming that he's going to be out for the evening with Mrs Lurinski, who has some explaining to do, so at zero hour myself, Ray and WPC Willems will present ourselves at the house of Stein, Duntocher Road, Bearsden. If he isn't there we'll proceed to the Lurinski household in Busby. Ray?'

'Sir?'

'Whether Stein is at home or not, I'd like you to ensure that we take the two samurai swords away with us. Evidence has been given to suggest that one of them is the murder weapon. Ensure that they are given to Dr Kay at Forensic first thing in the morning. We hope that there will still be traces of Lurinski's blood on the blade of one of the weapons.'

'Very good, sir.'

'Any questions?'

The room was silent.

'One more point: whoever arrests Stein, remember that he's likely to be carrying AIDS, so avoid unnecessary violence as I know you will anyway, but do so especially in this case, the minutest drop of his blood could be deadly.'

Chapter Eleven

Wednesday, April 3rd, 01.00–03.00 hours.

'Punt it in,' said Donoghue, and stood back as a hugely framed police sergeant of the uniformed branch put his shoulder to the door. The door splintered around the lock and the sergeant fell into the house. Donoghue and Sussock followed. Sussock groped for the light switch.

Mrs Stein was lying on the couch snoring loudly, a half-bottle of vodka in her hands.

'No wonder she didn't hear us,' growled the sergeant who had forced the door. 'It'd be easier to wake the dead than wake that.'

'Search the house, please,' said Donoghue, not at all caring for the sergeant's cold cynicism.

Ray Sussock took the swords off the wall and handed them to a young constable who slid them into a large plastic bag as other uniformed officers searched the house. 'Straight down to the station,' said Sussock, 'into the store, then down to Forensic first thing in the morning.'

'Very good, sir.'

'House empty, sir,' said the uniformed sergeant. 'Except for . . .' He nodded contemptuously at the stuporous Mrs Stein.

'All right. Can you post a man in the drive? Since we made the premises insecure we'll have to guard it until the lady wakes up, hopefully sober. It'll be up to her to call a joiner.'

'Yes, sir.'

The staff came out of the Zambesi at 01.30. They emerged in a group and walked up on to the pavement to where the taxis waited, ordered by the management to take the staff home. They stopped, surprised by the heavy police presence and obvious police interest in them. Those not challenged by the police stepped hurriedly past and into a taxi. Spike and Castlemilk Fats came up the stairs from the alleyway.

'Hi, boys,' said Montgomerie.

'Remember us?' said King.

'Just get in the van, please,' said Montgomerie.

If Donoghue had been a betting man he would have laid a large sum of money on the probability that Stein's flash Mercedes would be parked outside Mrs Lurinski's house.

He would have lost the bet. There was, he thought, just the possibility that he had left and driven back to Bearsden by another route and that they had missed each other. He thought it highly unlikely.

He left his car and, together with Ray Sussock and Elka Willems, walked up the driveway to the house of Lurinski. He pressed the doorbell. It gave just a simple two-tone ring. Chi Chu Lurinski answered it almost immediately and did not seem at all alarmed or surprised to see Donoghue standing there. In fact, it was hard for Donoghue to detect any emotion at all. She was wearing a black dress over which was a plastic apron.

'Yes,' she said. 'How can I help you?'

'We're looking for Rudolph Stein.'

'He's not here.'

'But you have seen him tonight?'

'Yes.'

'Do you mind if we come in and talk?'

She stepped aside. 'Can we talk in the kitchen? I'm preparing food.'

'Late to be working, isn't it? It's after two.'

'I'm a night bird,' she said, turning. The cops followed her into the kitchen. The kitchen was solidly built in pine, she had an eye-level oven and microwave. There was chicken meat on a cutting board. She picked up a cleaver and let it rise and fall on the chicken, dicing it into small pieces, letting the weight of the cleaver do all the work. 'I'm preparing a curry. I'll cook it tonight, let it cool, then heat it in the microwave for tomorrow's dinner. I've prepared three other meals tonight. It's how I work, cook five or six meals, freeze them, then heat them in the microwave when I want to eat them.'

'Very efficient,' said Donoghue.

'You can save a lot of time over the week,' Chi Chu Lurinski explained.

'So, Stein is not here?'

'No.'

'He was earlier?'

'No, he wasn't.'

'Mrs Lurinski, he was seen taking you to dinner.'

'I don't deny it. I said he wasn't here. I don't like the man, he makes me shudder. I wouldn't allow him in my house.'

'So why go to dinner with him?'

'Because he said he wanted to talk to me. Strictly business.'

'Did he?'

'Yes, nothing new, nothing he hasn't said before. He wants to buy me out, all three shops. He hinted that another fire could break out if I didn't, and since Samuel had been killed he wondered if I had changed my mind. He obviously thought Samuel was still nothing more than a business partner. He didn't know we had married. I didn't tell him otherwise.'

'What did you say to his proposition?'

'I said I would think it over, because I wanted him to take me home. He's also a little unstable, flies off the handle to say the least, so I dared not tell him there and then that I had no intention of selling out.'

'Have your visitors gone?'

'You saw them? Have you been watching me?'

'No, we've been watching Stein. We suspect him of your husband's murder.'

'I see. Well, my friends were just passing through Glasgow. They're really friends of my brother's, they heard about Samuel and called to give their condolences.'

'But they left?'

'Yes. Just after Rudolph Stein brought me back, in fact.' The cleaver rose and fell on the white meat.

There was a long, long silence. It was broken eventually by Donoghue, who said, 'So where have you left his body?'

But Chi Chu Lurinski just smiled and regretted that she did not know what the honourable Inspector of Police was referring to.

Phil Hamilton walked up Maryhill Road. It was 03.00 hours. A light drizzle fell. The city slumbered.

First he saw the car. A large Mercedes parked half on, half off the kerb. Two doors were open. He knew that it had been parked there in the last hour. It was also parked near the waste ground where almost forty-eight hours earlier he had found the headless corpse. Hamilton crossed the road and quickened his pace. As he reached the other side of the road he saw the mound lying beside the car.

Hamilton continued towards the car, a gnawing feeling of emptiness and dread growing inside him. He reached the car and switched on his torch, at the same instant he gripped the radio at his lapel.

He didn't recognize the man, but he saw clearly he was in middle age, grossly overweight, and apparently wealthy, going by the silk shirt and expensive suit. He was also very, very dead. He had sustained a number of stab wounds, but the lethal blow must have been the one to his throat, which had severed his windpipe and artery. At least this corpse had kept his head.

Hamilton switched off his flashlight and pressed

the send button of his radio. As he did so, he caught sight of a slight figure scurrying along the canal towpath.

Clarissa McIntyre was looking for her children, calling them in for their supper.